Enjoy all of these American Girl Mysteries®:

THE SILENT STRANGER   A *Kaya* Mystery

LADY MARGARET'S GHOST   A *Felicity* Mystery

SECRETS IN THE HILLS   A *Josefina* Mystery

THE RUNAWAY FRIEND   A *Kirsten* Mystery

SHADOWS ON SOCIETY HILL   An *Addy* Mystery

THE CRY OF THE LOON   A *Samantha* Mystery

SECRETS AT CAMP NOKOMIS   A *Rebecca* Mystery

MISSING GRACE   A *Kit* Mystery

CLUES IN THE SHADOWS   A *Molly* Mystery

THE PUZZLE OF THE PAPER DAUGHTER   A *Julie* Mystery

and many more!

— A *Kit* MYSTERY —

MIDNIGHT IN
LONESOME HOLLOW

by Kathleen Ernst

★ American Girl®

Questions or comments? Call 1-800-845-0005, visit our Web site
at **americangirl.com,** or write to Customer Service, American Girl,
8400 Fairway Place, Middleton, WI 53562-0497.

Printed in China
10 11 12 13 14 LEO 10 9 8 7 6

PICTURE CREDITS

The following individuals and organizations have generously
given permission to reprint illustrations contained in "Looking Back":
pp. 174–175—landscape, © Raymond Gehman/Corbis; grandmother and
child, Library of Congress; pp. 176–177—cabin, © Gary W. Carter/Corbis;
brochure cover, © Eastern National, Cumberland Gap National Historical
Park; dulcimer, © Gary W. Carter/Corbis; pp. 178–179—ballad collectors,
Cecil Sharp Photograph Collection, courtesy of the English Folk Dance and
Song Society, London, England; basket maker, photo by Doris Ulmann;
weaver, photo by Doris Ulmann; fabric samples, Collection of the Museum of
Early Southern Decorative Arts, Winston-Salem, NC; car in stream, Library
of Congress; Doris Ulmann with camera, © University of Kentucky, all rights
reserved, Special Collections and Digital Programs, University of Kentucky
Libraries; pp. 180–181—strip mine, © Karen Kasmauski/Corbis; coal miner,
Library of Congress; folk singers, Library of Congress; fiddler,
© Kevin R. Morris/Corbis.

Illustrations by Jean-Paul Tibbles

Library of Congress Cataloging-in-Publication Data

Ernst, Kathleen, 1959–
Midnight in Lonesome Hollow : a Kit mystery / by Kathleen Ernst ;
[illustrations by Jean-Paul Tibbles]
178 p.; 18 cm.
Includes historical information about Appalachian Mountain culture.
Summary: While staying with her Aunt Millie in the Appalachian Mountains of
Kentucky in the summer of 1934, Kit tries to discover who is sabotaging
a visiting folklore researcher.
ISBN 978-1-59369-161-5 — ISBN 978-1-59369-160-8 (pbk.)
[1. Mountain life—Kentucky—Fiction. 2. Appalachian Mountains—Fiction.
3. Aunts—Fiction 4. Depressions—1929—Fiction. 5. Kentucky—History—
20th century—Fiction 6. Mystery and detective stories.]
I. Tibbles, Jean-Paul, ill II.Title.
PZ7.E7315Mid 2007   [Fic]—dc22   2006047852

For Scott,
patron of the arts

TABLE OF CONTENTS

1

ON LONESOME BRANCH

Kit heard the stream's *swishy-whish, swishy-whish* song before she glimpsed it through the trees. "Isn't this Lonesome Branch, that leads to the Craig place?" she asked. "I've been looking forward to seeing Fern and Johnny all day."

"It sure is," Aunt Millie said. "Whoa, Serena!" The mule ambled to a halt on the steep trail. Aunt Millie looked down at Kit, who'd been walking beside the mule. "You've learned your way around these parts pretty well."

Kit grinned. "It's been fun visiting people with our traveling library!"

"This will be our last stop today," Aunt Millie said. "Climb up and hold on!" Kit swung into place on the mule and wrapped her arms around Aunt Millie's waist. Serena trotted down

1

the bank, splashed into the shallow water, and began picking her way upstream.

Kit sucked in a deep breath of mountain air, happy to be exactly where she was. She liked the way some of the isolated mountain families used creek beds as roads. She liked how the trees bent their branches over the waterways, making cool twilight from even a hot high-noon August day. Kit thought Kentucky's steep ridges and thick green forests were beautiful, but she also liked how sometimes—just some-times—she got a little shiver down her back while traveling far up a dark hollow.

Aunt Millie broke into Kit's thoughts. "It will be good to see how the Craigs are doing," she said. "Three children, living with just their grandmother—that's a hard row to hoe. They have all they can handle since Mrs. Craig died last year, especially now that Mr. Craig's gone to Detroit to look for work."

Kit sighed. The Great Depression was like a giant hand, reaching into even the most remote communities and cabins and squeezing tight.

Johnny and Fern's father had lost his job a year ago when the Mountain Hollow coal mine shut down. The mine owners had also closed the school where Aunt Millie used to teach. Kit and Aunt Millie had spent the last two weeks riding lumbermen's roads and mountain trails to bring books to the isolated families of Aunt Millie's former students—like the Craigs. Kit had never met Harlan, the oldest Craig child, but she liked the younger two.

"Fern and Johnny will be eager for new books," Kit said. Then she frowned, looking at the almost-empty canvas saddlebags. "I think Johnny's already read the only picture book we have left, though."

"Reading a book twice is better than not reading at all," Aunt Millie said briskly.

"And I saved a book for Fern," Kit added. "Did you know that her favorite book is *Robin Hood*? Just like me!"

Aunt Millie chuckled. "I knew you two would get along just fine. Johnny and Fern were two of my best students. I wish we could loan them a dozen books, but we just don't have enough! Well, there's no sense fretting over something that can't be helped."

Kit snorted. "I've never *once* heard you fret, Aunt Millie! Besides, I have a feeling that our traveling library is just getting started." She allowed herself a secret smile. She hadn't told Aunt Millie about her letters to friends in Cincinnati, asking them to send any books or magazines they could spare. Kit expected a package to arrive any day.

They traveled a mile or so upstream before emerging into a clearing. The Craig cabin sat against a steep slope, its huge squared chestnut logs weathered to a lovely silver. Fern and Johnny Craig sat on the porch with their grandmother and a neighbor. Kit recognized Mrs. Vesta Skidmore, a tall dark-haired widow with six children. Mrs. Skidmore had been singing in a strong, clear voice, but she stopped when she noticed the visitors.

After urging Serena up the creek bank, Aunt Millie paused politely outside the garden gate. "Hello!" she called.

Mrs. Craig shaded her eyes with a gnarled hand. "Come up and set down!" she called.

Kit slid to the ground as Johnny barreled from the porch. He wasn't more than six years old, but his hug almost knocked Kit over. "*Kit!* Did you bring me a book?"

Laughing, Kit resettled her big straw hat on her head. "We sure did! You may have read it before, but—"

"It doesn't matter," Johnny assured her.

Kit reached into the saddlebag. "Here you go. *The Little Engine That Could.*"

"I *love* this one!" Clutching his prize, he led the way toward the porch.

A fence made from what Kit called pickets, and her mountain friends called palings, surrounded the big garden by the cabin. As they walked past, Kit noticed that several palings needed to be replaced. A hoe blade broken from its handle lay on the ground, waiting for repair. *At least the garden itself is doing well*, Kit thought. She could see tomatoes hanging red and ripe, rows of lacy carrot greens marking the promise of growing roots, and squash and pumpkins developing on their spreading vines.

"Mamaw, look!" Johnny cried, waving his book in front of his grandmother, who was surrounded by basins and tubs heaped with green beans.

Auntie Craig's face, as wrinkled as a just-washed sheet, crinkled more as she regarded her grandson. "That's just fine," she said, touching his cheek with a tender hand. "And I surely want you to read it to me later. Right now, you go on and draw up a nice bucket of cold water and give our company a drink. Miss Millie, we don't have much, but we'll treat you clever. And Kit, too. How are you, honey?"

Kit paused. Auntie Craig's words were kind, but the old woman's usual energetic tone and broad grin were missing. "I'm fine, thank you," Kit said. "How are you, Auntie?" Mrs. Craig's grandchildren called her "Mamaw," but everyone else called her "Auntie Craig" as a sign of respect.

Auntie Craig looked at her lap. "We're getting by."

Kit greeted Mrs. Skidmore, then turned to Fern. "I brought a book for you, too! *Robinson Crusoe*."

"Thank you." Fern took the book but put it aside, ducking her head so her face was half hidden behind a curtain of wheat-colored hair.

Kit felt another poke of concern. *Something definitely isn't right here,* she thought. Fern was shy, but once the two girls had discovered their shared love of books, their previous visits had been full of giggles and chatter.

"I could start reading it out loud, while you work," Kit suggested.

Fern reached for a handful of beans. "I don't really feel like stories today," she said. "It was nice that you thought of me, though."

Kit and Aunt Millie exchanged a tiny frown. Then Kit waved her ever-growing scrapbook about Depression-beating tips. "Well, I brought my *Waste-Not, Want-Not Almanac,* too," she said. "Can you tell me what you're doing?"

She'd learned that in exchange for receiving a library book, people liked to share a recipe or a quilt pattern.

Auntie Craig mustered a little smile. "Why, we're just fixing up a mess of shucky beans," she said. "Miss Millie, you drag up a chair while I tell Kit how it's done."

Kit sat on the edge of the porch and wrote as Auntie, with demonstrations from Johnny, explained how to snap the ends from ripe green beans, pull out their tough fibery strings, thread the beans into long rows, and hang them up to dry. "Thank you," Kit said when she'd finished. "I'll suggest this to my mother when I get home." She sighed, leaning back against the porch rail. "I almost wish I could stay here forever! But I miss my family, and school starts in three weeks."

As soon as she'd spoken, Kit felt her face grow hot. Fern and Johnny's school near the mine was closed for good.

"It does make me mad as can be that those men who owned the mine just up and closed everything," Mrs. Skidmore muttered. "As if putting men out of work wasn't bad enough!"

"I tried to shame them into keeping the school open," Aunt Millie admitted. "But they wouldn't have it."

Mrs. Skidmore's thin face took on a fierce look. *Outsiders.* Our men worked themselves to nubs in that mine. And now the mine company is costing my kids an education. We need to organize ourselves to fight for a school, just like we did when the men formed unions and stood together to demand better wages and working conditions in the mines."

Kit thought about her own school, and had a sudden idea. "Maybe you could start a PTA!"

"What's that, honey?" Auntie Craig asked.

"A Parent-Teacher Association," Kit explained. "My school has one so parents and teachers can work together to solve problems."

Aunt Millie beamed. "What a wonderful idea! We'll call a meeting. Together, we might be able to think of something we can do!"

Kit jumped as a tired voice sliced through

the afternoon. "There ain't much you can do against a mine company. Or any other outsiders, either." A boy of perhaps seventeen had come around the house and stood by the porch steps. He wore patched trousers, a faded blue shirt, and a guarded expression.

"There *isn't* much you can do," Aunt Millie corrected calmly. "Good afternoon, Harlan."

This is Fern's brother? Kit thought, trying to hide her surprise.

"Harlan!" Auntie Craig scolded. "You greet these ladies proper."

Harlan stuck his thumbs under his suspenders and looked in turn to each of the women. "Miz Skidmore, Miss Millie."

Kit lifted her chin. "And I'm Kit," she said. "It's good to meet you." Harlan only nodded.

"Would you like us to save a book for you next time?" Kit asked.

Harlan met Kit's offer with a frown. "I don't want your books."

Fern pushed her needle through a green bean. "Where've you been, Harlan?"

"Just roaming up in the hills." Harlan shrugged. "I'll go split some wood and fill the wood box for you."

"I'd be kindly grateful," Fern said. Harlan walked away, and moments later a clear *thwack-thwack* echoed through the clearing as he began splitting logs into smaller pieces.

"That boy..." Auntie Craig shook her head. "He's a good one, but hard to harness."

Johnny blew out an impatient sigh. "What about the *school*?"

Aunt Millie chuckled. "Yes, let's return to the idea of forming a PTA. The sooner the better! As Shakespeare said, 'Nothing can come of nothing.' I still have a key to the schoolhouse so that I can keep an eye on it. If I held a meeting there, do you think parents would come?"

Auntie Craig looked away. "There's nothing I wouldn't do for these children, but sometimes it seems useless to keep trying."

"Auntie, we can't give up," Mrs. Skidmore said firmly. Then she looked at Aunt Millie. "How about tomorrow afternoon? I can send one of my boys around to give notice."

As the women worked out the details, Kit leaned close to Fern. "Is everything all right?" she whispered.

Fern bit her lip, and a sudden glint of tears appeared in her eyes. Finally she shook her head. "We've got trouble. But I can't talk about it now. Johnny doesn't know."

"I want to help!" Kit began, but Fern shook her head.

"Thanks, Kit. But I don't think there's any help for it." She slowly snapped a bean.

"Well, maybe if we talk about it together, we can think of something." Kit squared her shoulders. "May I come back sometime?"

For the first time that day, Fern met Kit's gaze. "I'd be pleased if you did," she said. "I get lonely, especially since the school closed. Come anytime, and spend the night if you want."

Kit put Harlan's rudeness out of her mind and nodded vigorously. "I'd like that!"

2

A Stranger Arrives

Kit's stomach was rumbling by the time she and Aunt Millie got home that afternoon. Since losing her teaching job, Aunt Millie had been living with her friend Myrtle Peabody, who'd also gladly made room for Kit. Miss Myrtle's tidy cabin nestled in a clearing among oak and hickory and chestnut trees, a three-hour mule ride up steep mountain roads from the nearest town. Two potted ferns prettied up the porch. A vegetable garden sprawled behind the home. The well stood in the side yard, and the outhouse farther back up the hollow. A much older cabin, long abandoned, was almost hidden from view on a wooded slope nearby.

Kit and Aunt Millie found Miss Myrtle sweeping the front porch. "I've got a soup kettle on the stove," she called.

"Supper smells wonderful, Miss Myrtle!" Kit exclaimed. "Today we visited Plum Branch and Apple Hollow and Blackberry Cove. It made me hungry! I'm going to start keeping a list of interesting place names in my Kentucky notebook."

Miss Myrtle chuckled. "That notebook of yours is growing fast. Any new words today?"

Kit considered. "Fern said 'kindly grateful' in a way I probably would have said 'kind of grateful.' It sounded much prettier her way."

"Learning about language is a good skill for a future newspaper reporter." Aunt Millie's voice was approving. She and her friend sat in straight-backed chairs and Kit settled into the porch swing. It made a *cre-ak, cre-ak* noise as she rocked, adding its wooden voice to the chorus of frogs and insects singing the sun down behind the ridges.

Aunt Millie told her friend about the day. "I feel more hopeful about teaching than I have in a long time," she said. "Perhaps we can find a new place to hold class sometimes."

"How about your old cabin on the hill?"
Kit asked Miss Myrtle.

"That old place?" Miss Myrtle shook her
head. "My great-grandpa built that one-room
cabin when he got married, but he and his
wife moved down here once they started a
family. No one's tended that cabin in years.
The roof's likely about to fall in."

"We'll think of something," Aunt Millie
declared. "The parents around here are worried
about their children's education. Surely we can
find a solution if we work together."

Remembering Auntie Craig's dejection, Kit
nodded slowly.

Miss Myrtle gave Kit a sideways look. "You
don't seem very excited."

"Something is troubling Fern and Auntie
Craig," Kit explained. "I'm trying to figure out
what they might be worried about."

"Probably food and clothes, like everybody
else," Miss Myrtle said.

Aunt Millie flicked a bit of dried mud from

her riding trousers. "Auntie Craig did seem distracted," she said. "But Kit, we mustn't pry."

"I'm not prying! Fern's my best Kentucky friend, and I like Johnny and Auntie Craig. I just want to help!" Kit shoved against the floorboards with her feet, making the swing move with extra vigor. "And then there's Harlan…" She tried to find a polite way to express her opinion of Fern's brother. "He didn't seem interested in our library at all."

"I don't know Harlan well," Aunt Millie mused, "so I don't know his interests. He came to class a few times when he was Johnny's age, but as firstborn, he had to help at home. And when Mr. Craig started working at the coal mine, he took Harlan with him."

"Harlan lost his job when the Mountain Hollow coal mine shut down," Miss Myrtle said. "He left home and managed to find work at one of the bigger mines that's still running. Those jobs are scarcer than hen's teeth these days! Harlan came back, though, empty-handed. Folks say he up and quit a paying job."

Kit was shocked to learn that Harlan had given up a good job. "Harlan said today that he didn't think it would do any good to try and work with the coal company men, or any other 'outsiders.' And Mrs. Skidmore used that word, too."

"Folks in these hills have good reason to be suspicious of outsiders." Miss Myrtle folded her arms emphatically. "We were raised to be hospitable. No one in these parts has enough to eat these days, but I've seen hungry people give away some of their own hard-earned corn or taters and not think twice! But too many strangers have taken advantage of simple kindness." She stared at the high ridges beyond her home. "Men from the outside come buy good folks' land for a few dollars, then turn around and make a quick fortune selling timber. And they leave a mess behind."

"When I was coming here on the train, I saw mountainsides that were nothing but stumps and weeds," Kit said, remembering how gloomy those barren slopes had looked.

"The same thing happens when companies buy mineral rights," Aunt Millie added. "The company owners often get rich while the men working in the mines struggle to get by."

Kit remembered also the look on Mrs. Skidmore's face when she spoke of the men working themselves "to nubs" in coal mines. "Do you think people see *me* as an outsider?" she asked slowly.

"Oh, I don't think so," Aunt Millie said. "Lots of folks remember your daddy. It's strangers that folks are cautious about, not kin who come to visit."

Kit wanted to feel reassured, but she noticed that Miss Myrtle didn't chime in. *I wouldn't even wonder about my welcome if Harlan had been more friendly*, she thought crossly.

Suddenly an unexpected flicker of movement through the trees down the slope in front of the cabin caught her eye. "Someone's coming up the lane," she said softly.

The three of them watched as a shadow emerged from the trees—a rider on horseback.

"Who is that?" Aunt Millie whispered.

Myrtle peered over her glasses and shook her head slightly. "I have no idea." She rose and walked to the porch steps.

The rider dismounted and marched to the front porch without waiting for an invitation. The stranger was a woman, dressed for riding in high boots and jodhpurs and a practical, broad-brimmed hat.

"I'm looking for Myrtle Peabody," she announced. "I've come to stay."

3
FERN'S WORRIES

For a moment no one seemed to know what to say. A nightingale's first evening song fluted through the silence.

"Oh dear. Please forgive me," the woman said. A startling wing of white streaked her black hair, and she used one hand to push back tendrils straggling loose from the coil of hair behind her neck. "My brother tells me I'm too direct for my own good. I'm Professor Lucy Vanderpool. I've come from Chicago, Illinois, to do some research. The storekeeper in town suggested that I talk to Myrtle Peabody."

"That's me," Miss Myrtle said, and then she introduced Aunt Millie.

"And this is my niece, Margaret Mildred

Kittredge," Aunt Millie added. She often called Kit by her full name.

Kit extended her hand. "It's good to meet you, ma'am," she said. "Most people call me Kit." Professor Vanderpool had a direct gaze and confident handshake that Kit admired.

"My soup pot's likely fit to boil," Miss Myrtle said, her tone reserved but polite. "Let's talk over supper."

While Professor Vanderpool tended her horse, Kit helped lay a simple meal of ham-bone soup and corn bread. *Miss Myrtle is as generous as they come*, Kit thought.

"Now," Aunt Millie said briskly when they were seated around the table. "What brings you to Kentucky, professor?"

"Oh please, do call me Lucy." Their guest smiled. "I'm a folklorist, and—"

"A *what*?" Kit asked, then added quickly, "Excuse me for interrupting."

"That's quite all right." Miss Lucy leaned forward intently. "Most people are unfamiliar with the type of work I do. *Folk* means people, of course, and *lore* has to do with all the knowledge and traditions people pass down. To put it simply, I'm interested in learning more about the mountain people of eastern Kentucky."

Aunt Millie looked skeptical. "That seems like a mighty tall order."

"And if you don't mind me asking," Miss Myrtle added, "why would a professor from Chicago travel all the way to Kentucky?"

"Folklore is such a big field that people often specialize," Miss Lucy explained. "Some learn about groups of people in city neighbor-hoods, or about people of a particular ethnic background. And some study certain topics, like food traditions or games. I'm here to learn more about the baskets made by people in this region."

Miss Myrtle looked startled. "Baskets?"

"Like that one." Miss Lucy pointed to an old basket sitting near the door.

Kit jumped up and fetched the basket. "We use this to gather eggs!"

"My mother made that basket, likely forty years or more ago," Miss Myrtle added. "I've used it for chores all this time. Why on earth would you want to study something like that?"

"More and more people are using tin pails and paper sacks to carry things in," Miss Lucy explained. "Basketry may well be a dying art."

Kit turned the basket over in her hands. It was large enough to hold a dozen eggs and was woven from thin strips of pale wood. "I'd never really noticed before," she said slowly, "but this *is* a pretty basket. The weaving is nice and even."

"That's exactly the type of detail I'm interested in!" Miss Lucy clasped her hands together, and Kit couldn't help smiling at her enthusiasm.

"So you want to look for other baskets?" Kit asked.

"Yes." Miss Lucy paused. "Mmm, this corn bread is delicious. I hope to document baskets and the people who made or use them. If you're willing, Mrs. Peabody, I'd love to photograph you with your mother's basket."

Miss Myrtle looked uncomfortable. "Well, now. I'll have to think about that."

"Of course," Miss Lucy said quickly.

"What got you interested in baskets?" Kit asked, hoping to smooth over the awkward moment.

"My parents moved from Kentucky to Chicago before I was born," Miss Lucy explained. "They brought one basket with them, a beautiful gathering basket made of white oak splits—"

"Splits?" Kit asked. Then she sighed as she realized that she'd interrupted again. "Sorry!"

Miss Lucy laughed. "Splits are these long, thin strips of wood used to weave this type of basket. It takes a lot of work to prepare them. My mother once told me that her basket was a gift from someone who lived near Mountain Hollow. My parents both died long ago, so I'm afraid I don't have any more information.

Unfortunately, basket makers don't sign their work, like painters do."

"Gracious!" Miss Myrtle snorted with laughter. "I can't imagine my mother putting her name on one of her baskets. It was just something she did, like mending clothes or planting a garden."

Miss Lucy nodded. "I understand. Nonetheless, from the looks of that basket, *I'd* say your mother was a skilled artist."

"Lots of people around here use baskets," Kit said, thinking back to the homes she'd visited in the past weeks.

"Not everybody makes them, though," Aunt Millie said. "The first person who comes to mind is Vesta Skidmore."

"I remember!" Kit said. "I noticed some nice ones when we visited her house."

"Is Mrs. Skidmore a friend of yours?" Miss Lucy asked hopefully.

"Well, Aunt Millie and I have been visit-ing folks because we kind of set up a visiting library," Kit explained. "Or as my friend Fern might say, 'We kindly set up a visiting library.'"

Miss Lucy looked surprised. "Are you taking note of local sayings, Kit? If so, then you're something of a folklorist yourself!"

"Why don't you show Miss Lucy your scrapbook and notebook?" Aunt Millie suggested.

Kit fetched her books. "I didn't expect a college professor to look at these," she said with a little self-conscious shrug. "Aunt Millie inspired me to start the scrapbook because she's so good at pinching pennies and making beautiful things out of almost nothing. All the people I've met in Kentucky this summer have given me new tips and ideas."

"I can see that," Miss Lucy said. She turned the pages slowly, looking at dried plants, bits of hand-dyed yarn, recipes, sketches of quilt patterns, and instructions for making soap.

"And I love to write," Kit explained. "When I hear new words or phrases, I write them in this notebook."

Miss Lucy pursed her lips thoughtfully as

she studied Kit's notes. "This is quite impressive, Kit."

Kit felt a flush of pride clear to her toes. "Thank you, ma'am."

Miss Lucy closed the notebook and sat back in her chair. "First, let me thank you all for the lovely supper. Mrs. Peabody, the storekeeper told me that you sometimes take in travelers. Are you willing to let me stay here for a few days while I visit families in the area? I would, of course, pay for room and board."

Miss Myrtle hesitated, glancing at Aunt Millie and Kit. Miss Lucy was a stranger, and her presence would make the cabin more crowded. But Kit liked the folklorist, and she knew that Miss Myrtle would welcome a few extra dollars. "There's always room for one more!" Kit said.

Aunt Millie smiled in agreement, and Miss Myrtle nodded. "I figure it's a go, then," she told the professor.

"Wonderful!" Miss Lucy said. "Now, I have another favor to ask. The student planning to travel with me came down with influenza. She wasn't going to get paid, but she wanted the experience, and I was counting on her help. Kit, would you be interested in working with me?"

Kit bounced on her toes. "I'd love to!" she exclaimed. "That is—if you don't think it will hurt our traveling library, Aunt Millie."

"At the moment, every book I have is already on loan," Aunt Millie reminded her. "It's not every day you get a chance to work with a college professor, Margaret Mildred! I think it's a jim-dandy idea."

❧

The next morning, Miss Lucy saddled her horse right after breakfast. "My equipment is in town," she explained. "I didn't want to pay someone to drive it up here until I was sure I had a place to stay."

"What kind of equipment?" Kit asked.

"You'll see." Miss Lucy's eyes twinkled as she swung into the saddle. "Don't forget—

please mention my project to Mrs. Skidmore today, if you have a chance."

Aunt Millie stepped onto the porch, her coffee cup cradled in her hand, as their guest disappeared down the road. "Do you need me today, Aunt Millie?" Kit asked. "Fern Craig invited me to come back. If I'm going to be busy with Miss Lucy, today might be the best chance I have."

"That sounds fine," Aunt Millie said. "Just don't stay too late. Men hardened by bad times tend to come out when the sun goes down. Moonshiners and the like. Most of the moonshiners are good men, trying to earn a few dollars to buy shoes for their children. But sometimes, there's trouble."

Kit had heard of the homemade whiskey called moonshine, and she wasn't interested in meeting any of the men who set up stills back in lonely hollows to make their brew. "I promise, Aunt Millie. I want to attend the PTA meeting this afternoon anyway."

After helping clean up the breakfast dishes,

Kit headed back toward Lonesome Branch. She hadn't gone far when she met Mr. Tibbets, the local postman, who traveled his route on horseback. His weathered face split into a slow smile when he saw her. "Miss Kit! If I'm not mistaken"—he patted one of his bulging saddlebags—"I believe I have a package with your name on it."

"Oh, boy!" Kit cried. "I bet it's books from Cincinnati!"

"Shall I dig it out now?" Mr. Tibbets asked.

Kit considered. "No, I don't want to haul a heavy package all the way to Fern's place and back. But Mr. Tibbets, I wanted to surprise Aunt Millie!" She thought fast. "Do you know where the old cabin is on Miss Myrtle's place? Could you leave the package there?"

"Sure." Mr. Tibbets whistled to his mare, and they started back down the lane. "Oh, and Kit," he added over his shoulder, "if there are any detective stories in there, I'd be grateful if you saved one to loan to me!"

FERN'S WORRIES

Kit found Fern, Johnny, and Auntie Craig once again up to their elbows in beans. Fern's face lit up. "It surely is good to see you, Kit! I didn't know if you'd truly want to come."

"Of course I wanted to come!" Kit protested. She carefully stepped over a row of roots left to dry on the porch floor before plopping down in the shade. "Are these for dyeing wool?" she asked, touching the shriveled roots. "This one almost looks like a little person with arms and legs!"

"Why, that there's just an old 'sang root," Auntie Craig told her.

Johnny puffed up with importance and corrected, "Teacher calls it ginseng."

"It'll fetch a good price down in the valley," Fern explained. "Folks say the Chinese use it as an herbal tonic. I walk down to the store from time to time and sell ginseng, or sassafras roots for tonic and tea. Sometimes we have a few extra eggs to sell. I can't steal time for a traipse like that 'til we get these beans up, though."

"May I help?" Kit asked, reaching for a handful of beans. "I hope you don't mind me coming back so soon, but I want to go to that PTA meeting this afternoon. And after today, I'm going to be busy." As they worked, Kit told the others about Miss Lucy.

"Come all this way to study on baskets?" Auntie Craig shook her head. "What some people do!"

"I'm glad she's studying baskets," Kit said. "I think she's right. Lots of people don't real-ize how talented they are! Since coming to Kentucky, I've seen beautiful quilts and hand-carved toys and baskets—all those things should be appreciated."

"Well, it seems peculiar to me," Auntie Craig said. "But if you want some talent, Fern here has a purty voice." The old woman's face looked proud. "The finest in all Kentucky, I'm certain."

Fern's cheeks turned tomato red. "Oh, Mamaw! It's nothing to speak of."

"It surely is," Auntie Craig insisted. "If I

couldn't hear you sing every day, why, I just don't know—" The old woman's voice quavered, and Kit shot a concerned glance her way. Auntie Craig managed a smile and continued, "If you don't want to sing, Fern, play Kit a song."

"Oh, please?" Kit begged. "I'd love to hear."

Fern bit her lip, then got up and went inside the cabin. A moment later she returned carrying an instrument Kit didn't recognize. It was larger than a violin, with the same hourglass shape, but longer and narrower. Fern sat in a chair and placed the instrument across her lap. She strummed the strings with a turkey quill held in her right hand as her left hand slid a small piece of wood up and down one of the strings to create different notes. The music Fern made was sweet and simple, yet somehow it reached inside Kit and vibrated there.

"That was beautiful!" Kit cried when the song ended. "What are you playing?"

"It's just a dulcimer," Fern said. Her embarrassment had faded to a soft shade of pink.

Auntie Craig nodded. "Fern has a gift with the dulcimer." She pronounced the word "dulcy-more."

Johnny tossed a bean into a tin basin with a satisfying *pling.* "I guess you didn't bring me a new book today," he said.

"I'm sorry, Johnny. Aunt Millie and I are plumb out." Kit tossed a bean after Johnny's, then sat up straight as a new thought popped into her brain. "I just got an idea! Maybe we could have a talent show and raise money for library books! Fern, you could play your dulcimer, and I could recite a poem, and—"

"Oh, no!" Fern said quickly. "Play in front of a group of people—no, I couldn't."

"But…" Kit began, then let her voice trail away. She had no right to push Fern. "I understand," she said more quietly. "And I'm ever so honored that you played for me. Thank you, Fern."

"It was a good idea," Auntie Craig told Kit

as Fern took her dulcimer back inside. "But most folks wouldn't have a penny to spare anyways."

"So no more books," Johnny said glumly.

"I've got other plans," Kit assured him. "In fact, a package just came in the mail. If there's a book in there I think you'll like, I'll set it aside for you."

Johnny's face brightened. "Really?"

"Really," Kit promised. "If you happen to see my Aunt Millie, though, don't say anything about it. I thought it would be fun to surprise her. Mr. Tibbets promised to hide the package for me in that old cabin near Miss Myrtle's place."

Just then Harlan appeared in the doorway. He had dark smudges beneath his eyes, as if he hadn't gotten enough sleep, and his hair hadn't been combed. *Did he just get out of bed?* Kit wondered. *I bet Auntie Craig and Fern have been working for hours!*

"Johnny," Harlan barked as he slapped a worn cap down on his head. "I could use your help fixing that chicken roost."

"All right." Johnny jumped to his feet and followed his older brother toward the barn.

"Don't nail it too close to the stalls," Auntie called after them. When Harlan didn't answer, she sighed and pushed to her feet. "I better see to it myself," she said. "Fern, honey, go check on that pan of corn bread I put in the oven."

Kit trailed Fern into the cabin, eager for a few minutes alone with her friend. The front room was tidy, with everything in its place. *Not a book of their own in sight,* Kit thought sadly, but Fern's pretty dulcimer hung on one wall in a place of honor. Asters and wild bergamot bloomed in a tin-can vase, and several pieces of artwork that Johnny had probably brought home from school graced the walls. The room was cheerful, somehow, even if the furnishings were simple and few.

"What's this?" Kit asked, distracted by an unusual lamp sitting on a shelf. A silver reflector almost hid the lamp itself, which was round and made of metal.

Fern checked the stove, then joined Kit. "That's my daddy's old carbide lamp. He wore it on his helmet when he worked in the mine."

Kit's forehead wrinkled. "How does it work?"

"Simple." Fern showed her that the lamp base had two chambers, one above the other. "My daddy explained it to me. You put crumbles of a rock called calcium carbide in the bottom, and water in the top. When water drips down on the rocks, it creates a stream of gas. Strike a match, and the gas will light. Then this reflector helps shine the light around." She positioned the lamp back on the shelf, just so. "I keep this one here because it reminds me of my daddy. But Harlan's got one too."

Kit hesitated. "Harlan looked tired," she began.

Fern looked up, and Kit saw that the worry had returned to her friend's blue eyes. "You saw it too?" Fern asked. "He—he's been looking like that lately."

"Maybe he's just been working too hard," Kit said, although she had trouble believing it.

"Well, I don't know about that." Fern shrugged. "Truth is, me and Johnny do most of the chores around here."

Kit glanced over her shoulder before speaking. "Does that bother you?" She hoped she wasn't giving offense.

Fern, though, surprised Kit by shaking her head. "No," she said simply. "That's just how it is. Harlan's always had a powerful need to wander. He loves these hills. But don't you judge him mean! He wants to do right by this family. He's not real talky, and I know folks think he's shiftless. But he's not a bad person."

"I'm sure that's true," Kit said, although in her mind she could hear Miss Myrtle's quiet voice from the night before: *Folks say he up and quit a paying job.*

Fern leaned closer. "He's been going out nights, though," she said. "For weeks, now, I've heard him creep out after dark, and then slide back in later."

"Have you asked him where he goes?" Kit asked.

"I tried, but he plain won't talk about it. He's been snappish as a treed coon ever since…" Fern's voice quivered, and she swiped at new tears with one hand.

"Oh Fern, what happened?" Kit asked. "I truly don't mean to pry, but if there's anything I can do to help, anything at all—"

"You can't help us." Fern sniffled and took a deep breath before looking at Kit straight on. "A county man came 'round day before yesterday, asking a bunch of questions. He told Mamaw that if she couldn't keep me and Johnny fed proper, he'd have to take us off to an orphanage."

"What?" Kit gasped. Auntie Craig's heart would break if Fern and Johnny were sent to an orphanage, and theirs would too. "Oh Fern, no!"

"I can hardly bear to think on it," Fern whispered.

Kit's mind was racing. "We should talk to

Aunt Millie. She might—"

"No!" Fern said fiercely. "Don't tell anyone. I'd be purely ashamed to have word get around that we Craigs can't take care of ourselves. Promise?"

"I—I promise," Kit stammered reluctantly.

"We're doing all right!" Fern insisted. "Our garden's come in real good this year. We still have a few chickens and a milk cow, and we'll gather grapes and hickory nuts this fall."

But you can't gather new shoes, or a new dress, Kit thought. Fern's yellow cotton dress was faded and threadbare.

"Harlan told that man that he already had a plan to earn some cash before snowfall," Fern was saying. "Now I'm scared that Harlan's gotten mixed up in some kind of trouble, trying to make money. I don't know why else he'd sneak out at night."

Kit squeezed Fern's hand, but as they went back to the porch, she remembered Aunt Millie's warning. "Fern... do you think

Harlan might be working with some moon-shiners, making whiskey?"

"Oh, no." Fern shook her head firmly. "Before Mother died, she made Harlan promise that he would *never* get mixed up with any moonshine business, no matter how lean times got. He promised her, Kit, and I know he meant it true."

Kit remembered the cold look in Harlan's eyes and wasn't so sure. *Either way, his sneaking about at night is making Fern worry,* Kit thought. And Fern had plenty of worries without her older brother adding more.

Kit felt a shiver slide down her spine. Suddenly, the mountains staring down at the little farm in Lonesome Hollow seemed full of secrets.

4
A SAD DISCOVERY

By the time Kit arrived at the schoolhouse
that afternoon, a dozen children were racing
around the yard. Kit paused, tempted to join
the fun, but then turned to the door and
slipped inside.

"Thank you all for coming," Aunt Millie
was saying. She stood by the blackboard.
Several women had squeezed into the student
desks. One was rocking a baby, and another
was keeping an eye on a toddler who seemed
entranced by the colorful map on the wall.

"Mrs. Vance isn't here, or the Maggards,"
Aunt Millie continued. "Does anyone know if
they're coming?"

"No ma'am, they aren't," said one of Mrs.
Skidmore's sons. Roy Skidmore was a skinny,

sunburned boy of about ten, standing with hands shoved into his overall pockets. "Mrs. Vance said she needs all her young'uns at home to help with chores, so there wasn't any point in coming. The Maggards are fixing to move to Louisville so Mr. Maggard can find work."

"I came out of respect, Miss Millie," the woman with the toddler said. "But I can't let my kids away from chores, either."

"Seems to me the problem isn't just letting the children loose to come to school," a woman named Mrs. McCorkle said. "None of us can afford books or paper or pencils to send with 'em."

"Perhaps we could write to the mine company owners," someone suggested. "They might be willing to send some supplies. It's the least they could do, seems like."

"I don't expect we should beg charity from outsiders," Mrs. Skidmore said firmly. She had brought some knitting with her, and her needles seemed to *clickety-click* in soft agreement.

Kit sighed as everyone began to chatter

at once. She was heartsick about the threat to Fern's family, and now Aunt Millie's hopes of finding a creative solution to the problem of educating the local children seemed as forlorn as the abandoned coal-mine operation outside. Kit looked out the window. Beyond the children playing marbles and tag, the once-bustling Mountain Hollow coal mine was silent. In the scarred hillside, rusting coal cars, and sagging shacks, Kit could see the ghosts of a mine that had helped feed many local families. But those days were gone.

Suddenly, an unexpected movement caught Kit's eye. She leaned closer to the window. There—someone slid from the shadows of an abandoned shack, then darted quickly behind the next building.

"Aunt Millie!" Kit blurted. She flushed as everyone turned to look at her. "I—I thought I saw someone, over by the mine buildings."

"Probably one of our men cutting through," Mrs. Skidmore said. "Someone hunting."

"Probably!" Kit agreed brightly, then turned

back to the window. She hadn't seen a gun in the young man's hands. What she had seen was a slight figure in worn trousers, with dark suspenders plain against a faded shirt and a battered cap pulled low over his forehead. Loyalty to Fern had kept Kit from saying more, but she was certain that the young man she'd seen slipping stealthily through the abandoned mine camp was Harlan Craig.

❦

The PTA meeting ended without a plan to reestablish regular classes. Everyone agreed, though, that the idea merited more discussion.

"We've got to stick together in these hard times," Mrs. Skidmore told Aunt Millie as the women headed outside to gather their children. "That'll see us through."

Kit, distracted with wondering about Harlan Craig, suddenly remembered her assignment from Miss Lucy. "May I have a moment, Mrs. Skidmore?" she asked.

"Why, surely, child," Mrs. Skidmore said.

"Roy, you go round up the little ones so we can start home."

Kit explained the folklore project. "Miss Lucy is really nice," Kit added. "She'd like to meet you, if you'd be willing."

Mrs. Skidmore considered. "Myrtle's place isn't far outten the way of our walk home. How about we stop by, and I'll meet your Miss Lucy? Then we'll see."

Aunt Millie overheard. "Don't wait for me," she said. "I'm going to dust the schoolroom. No sense in wasting an opportunity."

Kit smiled. Trust Aunt Millie to make the most of her trip to the school!

As they walked to Miss Myrtle's house, Kit fell into step with Roy. "Thanks for spreading the word about the meeting," Kit said. "I know Aunt Millie appreciates it."

For a moment Kit thought Roy was too shy to answer. Finally he said, "I hope Teacher can find a way to hold class again. I especially liked science. Once we studied about weather."

"Aunt Millie will figure out something," Kit

said. "She's not one to let the Depression win!"

When Kit and the Skidmores reached Myrtle's home, they found the folklorist lugging crates and suitcases from the front porch, where her driver had deposited them, into the house. Kit quickly made the introductions.

"My baskets are simple things," Mrs. Skidmore said flatly. "I don't imagine they'd be of much interest to a professor from Chicago."

"Oh, but they would!" Miss Lucy insisted.

Mrs. Skidmore folded her arms. "Kit here says you want to photograph me with my baskets. Would you want me to put on my granny's old dress or drag a spinning wheel down from the attic?"

Miss Lucy looked startled. "Why would I do that?"

"A fellow came through here a few years ago taking pictures," Mrs. Skidmore said. "He wanted everybody to dress in old clothes and pose with stuff long since tossed aside. If you're trying to make people look like quaint, old-fashioned hillbillies, I want no part of it."

Miss Lucy looked her straight in the eye. "I want to show how people make and use their baskets," she said firmly. "I believe basketry is a skill that is in danger of disappearing, and I'd like to help preserve that skill. Nothing more."

Kit watched Mrs. Skidmore consider that. The youngest Skidmore girl squatted down to study a caterpillar inching past. Kit crossed her fingers behind her back.

Finally Mrs. Skidmore nodded. "Come by tomorrow," she said. "Kit here knows the way."

"Wonderful! But…" Miss Lucy hesitated. "I have some equipment, you see. Too much to bring on horseback, and I haven't had a chance to hire a car or wagon around here."

Mrs. Skidmore snorted. "Few in these parts have cars. But I'll send Roy 'round in the morning with a wagon, if that'll suit."

"Perfect!" Miss Lucy clasped her hands in that joyful manner of hers. Mrs. Skidmore was already marshaling her brood down the lane.

"See you tomorrow!" Kit called after them.

She was pleased when Roy paused to give her a little wave.

Miss Lucy put a hand on Kit's shoulder. "Thank you, Kit. Sometimes those first introductions into a community can be the hardest."

"Mrs. Skidmore's a widow," Kit said. "I think she's had a rough time. But I'm pretty sure she's decided she likes you."

"Good." Lucy turned toward her crates. "Now, would you like to see what I brought?"

Kit followed her up the steps and peeked inside one of the boxes. "Oh—a typewriter!" She grinned. "I've had some practice with one of those."

"You have?" Miss Lucy's eyebrows arched in surprise. "Wonderful! How about this?" She gently eased the lid from another crate.

Kit peered inside. "It looks like a camera— but it's bigger than any camera I've ever seen!"

Miss Lucy gently pulled the bulky camera from its padded crate. "This one's very old. The folklore department at my college can't afford new cameras, I'm afraid. But I don't mind making do." She laughed. "My brother Pete tells me I need to keep up with the times, but I've grown rather fond of this camera."

"Is your brother a folklorist too?" Kit asked.

"Heavens, no!" Miss Lucy shook her head. "He's in the music business, and he's always interested in the latest ideas. He teases me by saying that while he looks forward, I'm busy looking backward, using old equipment and trying to document basket-making traditions before they disappear."

Kit was still studying the camera. "Where does the film go?"

"This camera uses glass plates instead of film to make the images." Miss Lucy showed Kit the glass plates she'd brought, each carefully wrapped to protect it from light. "Each plate holder has room for a piece of clear glass, which will capture the photograph, and a dark slide, which protects the glass from light until I'm ready to take the picture."

"This seems like a lot of equipment," Kit observed. In addition to the camera and glass plates, Miss Lucy had brought two different lenses and a tripod to steady the big camera.

"It is. But I've learned how to make good pictures with this equipment, Kit." Miss Lucy gave Kit a conspiratorial smile. "I don't want to just record what baskets look like. I want to make truly beautiful photographs of baskets and their makers."

Kit grinned. "That sounds wonderful!"

"I'll send copies of the portraits to people who allow me to study and photograph their baskets," Miss Lucy added, "as a small thank-you for their help. Won't that be grand?"

"Yes, ma'am!" Kit said. She could hardly wait to get started.

❧

That evening, Kit pushed her tired legs to climb the hill on the east side of Miss Myrtle's cabin. Trees cast long shadows, and mindful of the fading light, she tried to hurry. Miss Myrtle had been right about the old Peabody cabin: one corner of the roof had fallen in, and the single window cut into the front wall was empty of glass. The door hung partially open, and Kit was relieved to see that Mr. Tibbets had left her parcel just inside, propped against the wall.

Kit dropped to her knees. The package was stained and torn, as if every postman along the way had dropped it, scuffed it in the mud, or peeked inside. "You'd think the mail was kicked here from Cincinnati," Kit muttered as she quickly pulled the wrapping paper aside.

Then her shoulders sagged—and her spirits with them. Her Cincinnati friends had sent donations for the traveling library, all right. But someone had ripped the magazines apart. Pages fluttered from the books. Harsh pencil scribbles scarred the cover of a fairy tale.

"Why would anyone do such a thing?" Kit whispered, but the only response was a cricket chirping from a shadowed corner. Her hands clenched into fists, and tears stung her eyes. The library books were ruined.

5

AN UNEXPECTED THREAT

Kit had given her cot upstairs to Miss Lucy and had made a nest for herself in a storage room next to the kitchen. She hid the battered books behind a potato barrel, but as she lay staring into the darkness that night, she couldn't get them out of her mind.

Who would destroy books? Surely not Mr. Tibbets, the postman. But no one else knew about the package! Well, except Fern and Johnny. Kit had told her friends about the books that morning—

Suddenly Kit sat up straight. Harlan had come to the door as Kit talked to Fern and Johnny on the porch. He had certainly heard her talking about the package of books.

"Would Harlan be so mean?" Kit

whispered. If so, was it because he saw her as an outsider? Something cold and sad settled beneath her ribs. Why wasn't Harlan worried about what *really* mattered—keeping his family together?

Kit lay back down, but it took a long time to go to sleep.

❧

First thing the next morning, Kit picked up Miss Myrtle's oak split basket and went outside to gather eggs. She usually loved this chore, relishing the pearly light of dawn, the cool dew beneath her bare feet, the spanking-bright promise of a new day. But today she felt tired. She glanced back at the cabin and saw Aunt Millie through the window, bustling about the kitchen. Kit longed to tell Aunt Millie about the county worker threatening to take Fern and Johnny from their home, and about her suspicions of Harlan. But she'd made Fern a promise. And although she couldn't think who else besides Harlan might have destroyed the library books, she couldn't *prove* he'd done it, either. Sighing, Kit got on with her chore.

After breakfast, Kit helped Miss Lucy prepare for their day "in the field," as Miss Lucy called it. "Always use one of these notebooks with blue bindings for your notes," Miss Lucy told her. "And I'll use one of these with a red binding to keep a record of what photograph I take where."

They put two notebooks and two pencils into a leather satchel. Extras were stored next to carefully wrapped glass plates in a crate that they hauled out to the Skidmores' wagon.

"Mornin', Kit," Roy said.

Kit gave Roy her warmest smile. "Good morning!" she responded, and thought, *At least Roy likes me.* The boy seemed shy of the folklorist, avoiding direct eye contact and stepping back respectfully as Miss Lucy approached the wagon. Kit wondered if it was Miss Lucy's unusual task or her bustling energy that kept Roy tongue-tied.

Kit and Miss Lucy sat in the back of the

wagon with the precious camera braced between them. By the time the wagon jounced into the Skidmores' yard, Kit was sure she was going to be bruised black-and-blue. Miss Lucy didn't seem to mind the rough transport, and Kit admired her spirit.

The Skidmore home was made of mill-sawn boards instead of logs. Kit could see Roy's brothers at work in the cornfield, and a sister busy in the garden. Mrs. Skidmore was on the front porch working on a basket with one of her daughters. They sang as they worked, their voices ringing through the morning.

"Oh, I wish my brother could hear this," Miss Lucy murmured.

Mrs. Skidmore beckoned when she noticed her company. "Come on up where it's shady."

"Oh my gosh, Mrs. Skidmore," Kit exclaimed when she got close enough to see the baskets Roy's mother had lined up on the porch. "Look at this striped one!"

Mrs. Skidmore picked up the multicolored

basket Kit had admired. "I wove honeysuckle and willow in with the oak splits to make that pattern. And this one has strips of hickory bark woven in. I'll sell these down to one of the craft shops, where tourists come."

"They're gorgeous," Miss Lucy said. "Now, it will take me a few moments to get organized. I can call you when we're ready, if you'd like. I know you're busy."

Mrs. Skidmore regarded Miss Lucy with an expression that just might, Kit thought, hold a hint of approval. "That'll suit."

While Miss Lucy unpacked the camera, Kit settled down with a sharp pencil and one of the blue-bound notebooks. "I need you to record the name, date, and place," Miss Lucy explained. "Make note of any other important information, such as whether the baskets we study were made by the owner, inherited, or purchased."

"Got it," Kit said.

When they were ready to begin, Miss Lucy asked Mrs. Skidmore to explain her interest in basket making. "Is it something you've done all your life?" the professor asked.

"Well, no." Mrs. Skidmore reached for a new split. "My parents bought what baskets they needed from Elmer Crabtree. Old Elmer used to put a string of baskets over his shoulder and walk from farm to farm, selling them."

"Is this Elmer Crabtree still alive?" Miss Lucy's voice was hopeful.

Mrs. Skidmore shook her head. "No, he died years ago. His son still lives on the old homeplace, though. He could show you some of his father's work."

Elmer Crabtree, Kit wrote, putting a star by his name. *Used to sell baskets.* She tried to find a balance between scribbling furiously to keep up and leaving a neat record. *Need to visit the Crabtree homeplace.*

Mrs. Skidmore began to carefully weave the long oak split between the ribs of her basket, over-under, over-under. "Anyway," she said, "after I had a family of my own, we lived for three years in one of the big mining camps south of here while my husband dug coal. I didn't have a farm to tend, just a tiny little box of a house to keep. I had time on my hands, and too much to worry about."

"Because the Depression had started?" Kit asked. She understood all too well what kind of worries the Depression had brought.

Mrs. Skidmore paused, staring at the basket. Suddenly she began to sing:

When a rich mine boss finds
A mountain man for hire,
He pays him almost nothing,
Calls him "hillbilly" and "briar."

My husband never sees the sun.
He works with many dangers,
Digging out the coal to heat
The homes of perfect strangers.

Mrs. Skidmore sang several more verses. Her voice was not pretty, but it held a strength and power that seemed to quiver in the air.

And the words to the song gave Kit a new glimpse of how hard a miner's life was. Did the electricity in *her* Cincinnati home come from coal dug by Kentucky miners?

When Mrs. Skidmore finished singing, no one spoke for a long moment. Kit heard one of the boys calling the other from the field, and a blue jay scolding from the fence. "Those were some hard times," Mrs. Skidmore said finally. "I started making baskets there, to keep busy. I taught myself," she added, and although her voice was quiet, Kit recognized the satisfaction Roy's mother took in her work.

"With your permission, I'd like to make a series of photographs showing you at work on a basket," Miss Lucy said. "Roy, would you be willing to help?"

Roy hesitated, looking as if he thought the strange equipment might bite him. "Roy Skidmore," his mother said sternly, and he shrugged and nodded.

Over the next hour, Mrs. Skidmore demonstrated how she used an ax to shape the ribs of the basket, how she split lengths of oak into narrow weaving material, and how she began to shape a basket. Kit was so fascinated that she had to remind herself to describe the process as best she could in her notebook.

Miss Lucy periodically cried, "Stop! I *must* capture this!" She'd place her camera on its tripod and duck under the heavy black cloth she used to block out background light while she composed the photograph. Then she closed the lens shutter, positioned the glass plate, and had Roy press the cable-release button to take the picture.

After the demonstration, Mrs. Skidmore looked at Miss Lucy. "Well, now. Is that what you wanted?"

"That is exactly what I wanted," Miss Lucy said fervently. "*Thank you.* I'm impressed with not only your technical skill but also with your ingenuity and artistry. Almost all the baskets I've studied so far have been made of oak splits. But you've used a variety of materials."

Kit picked up a basket that was just the

right size for carrying home groceries. "This one has wire woven in." The strands of silver added a beautiful glint to the basket—and, she guessed, made it even stronger.

"I don't like waste," Mrs. Skidmore said. "Last year, a crew blasted a road through down by Tinker's Run and left all kinds of odds and ends behind. I gathered up what I could find and put them to use."

When Miss Lucy had finished "documenting" the baskets, as she called it, she spent fifteen minutes deciding how to pose Mrs. Skidmore. Kit watched the folklorist stride back and forth, eyes narrowed, as she considered. "Shadows too long here," she muttered, or, "Not enough contrast." Kit, who had snapped photos on her brother's small camera without ever considering things like shadows or contrast, was intrigued.

Finally Miss Lucy posed Roy's mother on the front porch steps, surrounded by her handiwork. Then she settled on the ground in front of the house with her camera.

"Why not use the tripod?" Kit asked, perplexed.

Miss Lucy wriggled to the left, lining up the photograph just so. "With a portrait like this, I think it's respectful to be looking up slightly at my subject," she explained.

When the photograph had been taken, Miss Lucy promised to send a print after she returned to Chicago.

"That will be fine," Mrs. Skidmore said. "Now, it's near on to dinnertime, and no one leaves my house hungry." She called to her daughter, who'd been silently shaping her own basket. "Honey, Kit and Miss Vanderpool are staying to noon with us. Go inside and fix up some corn bread and beans."

Kit and Miss Lucy joined the Skidmore children inside, squeezing onto two benches at the white enamel-topped table in the main room. At the end of the meal, after a murmured instruction from her mother, one of the girls proudly fetched a tin box and offered each person a cookie. When Kit took a bite, she found a pleasing but unfamiliar mix of spices. "This is delicious!" she exclaimed.

"I got the recipe from an Italian woman I met in the mining camp," Mrs. Skidmore said. "She didn't speak much English, but we got to be friends."

"I'm glad you have at least one good memory from that time," Miss Lucy said carefully.

Mrs. Skidmore nodded. "Our years in the big camp were hard in many ways. But there were good things, too."

"I'm sorry the mine bosses were so mean!" Kit blurted out.

"Some bosses try to be fair," Mrs. Skidmore said. "Some don't. Those that don't—well, a body just has to stand up for what's right. My husband helped organize the miners, and they worked together to demand reasonable hours and fair pay. I wrote songs, and wove baskets to help keep food on the table. I've got a brain and two hands and a voice, and I figure the good Lord intended me to use them."

By the time the dishes were cleared away, Miss Lucy and Mrs. Skidmore were chatting like old friends. "Vesta," Miss Lucy said, "I need a driver. If you can spare Roy for a few days, I'll pay him for the job."

Roy hunched his thin shoulders. "I was fixing to ash the cabbage tomorrow," he said. "Before moths make trouble. And the fence needs—"

"I think we can manage," his mother told him. Miss Lucy looked relieved.

Kit carried the satchel out to the wagon. Roy followed and stood staring at the garden, his hands thrust into his pockets. A hammer dangled from a loop on his overalls, and bits of twine and several nails peeked from his shirt pocket. Kit hated seeing him so anxious about cabbage moths and sagging fences. "I'm sorry if helping Miss Lucy and me is taking you away from your chores," she said.

"I've got a lot to do," he burst out. "I promised Daddy I'd take a big hand in keeping the place going."

Kit sensed pride buried beneath Roy's worry. "Will you show me what you've got planted?" she asked.

After a moment's hesitation, Roy took her on a quick tour of the huge garden. "We've got sweet potatoes in this here front row," he said, pointing. "Mother likes the look of the vines. That patch is broom corn—we're hoping to sell that. Pole beans over here—oh, shoot, that pole's leaning." He used a piece of twine to secure one of the poles supporting the twining bean vines. "And corn and rye on those fields on the hill."

Kit whistled appreciatively. "This is a lot for you and your brothers to tend. And a lot of produce for your mother and sisters to preserve."

"I hole up most of it," Roy said.

"Hole up...?"

"You dig a hole," he explained. "Then you pack garden truck like turnips or cabbage down in straw, and cover it with dirt again. Everything keeps good all winter. It saves

Mother time to work on her baskets, and saves the cost of jars."

"I'll have to write that down," Kit said admiringly. "You're a natural-born farmer."

"My daddy taught me." Roy swallowed hard, looking over the gardens. "I guess he knew everything there was to know about farming. He knew that the best time to plant potatoes is a dark night in March, and he knew to give eggs to a cow that's gotten into poison ivy, and—" Roy's voice was rising, and he wiped his nose on his sleeve before continuing in a quieter voice, "and *everything*."

Kit hesitated. "Did your father get killed in a mine accident?"

Roy shook his head. "No. My daddy lost his job at the big mine camp when the Depression hit, so we came back to the homeplace."

"My dad lost his job when the Depression hit, too," Kit told him. "It was scary."

"We would have gotten by," Roy said. "But then Daddy... he got sick. And he up and died."

"I'm so sorry," Kit told him. She started to reach out her hand, but Roy's face was suddenly so bleak, so full of private pain, that Kit realized her gesture might be unwelcome. Just in time, she let her hand drop.

"That was an excellent start to my research," Miss Lucy said as they headed back down the lane. "And I'm anxious to visit Mr. Crabtree. Do you know the way, Roy?"

"Yup," he said. "But old Mr. Runyan's place is just east of here. I think his wife used to make baskets. We could stop there."

"Wonderful!" Miss Lucy said. "Thank you, Roy."

Roy drove for several miles before turning off on a lane so narrow that Kit had to duck away from branches reaching out to scratch her skin or snag her hair. A few minutes later, they emerged into a small clearing. An ancient, windowless log structure squatted on the slope.

Roy halted the wagon beside a weed-choked

garden, hopped down, and extended a hand to Miss Lucy. Kit smiled as she scrambled down after them, pleased that Roy was feeling more comfortable with the folklorist.

"Mr. Runyan's just about deaf," Roy said, leading them forward. When they reached the front step he shouted, "Hello!"

The door stood open, and Kit thought she heard shuffling footsteps. A man poked his head around the doorway. His hair needed trimming, and his long gray beard drooped to his waist. "Who's that?" he demanded.

"I got a lady here come all the way from Chicago!" Roy yelled. "She wants to—"

Mr. Runyan bounded out the door. *"Git!"* he bellowed.

Kit was too astonished to move. Miss Lucy took a hasty step backward and stepped on Kit's toes. "Ow!" Kit yelped, and for a moment it seemed they would both land sprawling.

"You heard me!" Mr. Runyan shouted. "I said to git offen my land!" He shook one fist in the air. "Or I'll throw you off myself!"

6

DOUBLE DISASTER

Back on the main road, Miss Lucy took a moment to tuck a few loose hairpins into place before speaking. "Not the reception I'd hoped for," she said finally. "From now on, I think we'll wait in the wagon until we're sure of our welcome."

Kit swatted at a hovering cloud of gnats. "That sounds like a good plan." She glanced over her shoulder, half-afraid Mr. Runyan had followed them, and was relieved to see nothing but the empty road.

In the next hour Roy stopped at several more homes. Each time Kit and Miss Lucy waited in the wagon while Roy explained their mission. And each time he walked back, shaking his head. "Sorry, ma'am," he said.

"They don't want to talk to you."

"Let's go on to the Crabtree place," Miss Lucy told Roy after the third disappointment. "If I tell Mr. Crabtree that your mother suggested I visit him, he might be willing to help me."

Once they were on their way, Miss Lucy leaned closer to Kit. "Do you know the Crabtrees?" she asked in a low voice. "I don't want to stir up resentment by stopping at places where we're not welcome."

Kit shook her head. "I've never met them. I think there's just Mr. Crabtree and his youngest daughter left at home. Talitha, that's her name."

Half an hour later, Roy reined in the horse at a spot where a creek curved near the road. He jumped down and looped the lines over a tree limb. "The Crabtree place is a mile or so up the branch."

Kit looked down the steep bank to the creek, which looked deep and fast. "How do we get there?" she asked.

Roy pointed. "There's a path on the other side. See that plank? We can cross the creek there, and then feet it the rest of the way to the Crabtree place."

Kit didn't mind walking a mile—or "feeting it" a mile, as Roy would say. But the plank looked mighty narrow. After eyeing the makeshift bridge, Kit squared her shoulders and lifted her chin. "Well," she said. "This looks like an adventure!"

"Want me to help carry your camera across?" Roy asked Miss Lucy.

She shook her head. "Absolutely not. I'll consider myself lucky if *I* get across the creek without getting wet."

Roy edged the wagon into the trees, and Miss Lucy tucked a tarp over the crates that cradled the camera and glass plates and extra supplies. Then Roy led the way down the steep embankment to the plank bridge. He crossed the creek with careless ease.

When Kit followed, she found that the plank bounced a bit beneath her weight.

"Yikes!" she cried, going stock-still as she watched the water rush by beneath her. For a moment she felt dizzy. Then she focused on Roy, waiting on the far side. One careful step at a time, she managed to edge across the plank successfully. It was a little scary—but exciting, too.

Then Miss Lucy stepped gingerly onto the plank. She stopped several times to catch her balance, windmilling her arms, and Kit held her breath. But Miss Lucy finally joined them, smiling triumphantly.

They followed a narrow path shaded by towering chestnut trees and sometimes crowded by shrubby magnolias and rhododendron bushes. Finally they emerged into a beautiful hollow framed by ridges rippling into the distance. The two-story, squared-log home was similar to many others Kit had visited, but she couldn't help staring at a small dead tree in the front yard. Someone had hung dozens of empty glass bottles—green, blue, red, yellow—from its branches. She'd seen mountain families pitch empty containers and such into a heap behind their homes, but never this strange method of discarding trash.

Roy was already heading up the porch steps. "Hello!" he hollered. He must have gotten an answer, for he turned and gestured for Kit and Miss Lucy to follow him inside.

Kit paused to admire cheerful red geraniums growing in old lard buckets set on the porch. Green vines twined around strings stretched from the porch floorboards to the roof, creating a lovely cool hideaway. "This place has a good feel," she whispered to Miss Lucy. The folklorist smiled and led the way into a sitting room.

"Talitha's in the kitchen," Roy called from the next room. "She said to come on in."

Talitha Crabtree sat at the table, busy with scissors and old newspapers. She was a young woman with black hair and eyes that sparkled like sunshine on a creek, but Kit's smile faded when she saw who was sitting across from Talitha.

Harlan Craig.

He stared at Kit coolly, giving no sign that they'd met before. Kit felt her face grow hot, but she met his gaze with her own. *I'm not afraid of you*, she tried to tell him silently.

Meanwhile, Roy made the introductions. "Welcome!" Talitha said. "I'm glad to know you. My daddy's napping just now, but he'll be up soon, and glad to talk with you. We've still got a lot of my grandpa's old baskets around the place."

"We don't mind waiting," Miss Lucy said eagerly. "And in the meantime, if I may ask… what are you doing?"

Talitha smiled. "Just fixin' up to repaper the walls in here. It helps keep the wind out. Besides, Daddy can't get around much anymore. At least I can change the scenery in here."

Kit examined one of the walls. Every piece of newspaper was carefully aligned. Pictures from catalogs provided cheery spots of color. Poems had been arranged over the sink. "I've seen people line their walls with newsprint before," she said admiringly. "But I've never seen it done so—so *artistically* before."

"Why, thank you." Looking pleased, Talitha spread flour-and-water paste over several clippings. Kit glanced at Harlan and was astonished to see that a look of longing had crept into those hard eyes as he watched Talitha. *My goodness!* Kit thought. *Is Harlan sweet on her?*

"Let me finish this bit, and I'll see to you proper," Talitha promised Miss Lucy.

Just then, a voice floated down the stairs. "Talitha?"

She jumped to her feet. "Daddy needs my help on the steps," she said, but paused, frowning down at her work. "Harlan, would you put those pieces up for me? Right there, on that blank spot." She indicated a piece of cardboard nailed to the wall near the stove.

Harlan's look of affection vanished. "Wall-papering is women's work," he complained.

Talitha, already at the door, turned and gave him a stern look. "Harlan Craig!" she

said. "I don't expect any boy who comes calling on me to fuss when I need a bit of help! I
clipped that story out special, and I don't want
it spoiled because the paste dries before it gets
up on the wall." With that she disappeared
into the front room. A moment later Kit heard
her footsteps hurrying up the stairs.

Silence settled over the kitchen. Kit and
Miss Lucy exchanged uncomfortable looks. "I
left my satchel on the porch," Miss Lucy said.
"Kit, why don't we go fetch it. And Roy, perhaps you could find us a dipper of water."

Outside, Roy headed to the well. "I believe
I'll take a stroll by the creek," Miss Lucy
murmured.

Kit hesitated, then scooted into the secluded
porch hideaway and pulled her own notebook
from the satchel. She would use this spare
moment to write down how the strings-and-
vines system shaded the porch so beautifully.
She didn't stop scribbling when she heard footsteps descend the stairs inside. But a moment
later Talitha's raised voice coming through the

open kitchen window made Kit freeze.

"Harlan!" Talitha cried. "Why did you do that?"

"I don't like women's work," Harlan growled.

"I never saw such meanness." Talitha's voice trembled. "You go on, now. Just get on home."

"Fine," Harlan said. "I will. But listen—" His voice dropped. "You shouldn't help that woman out there. She's an outsider, and that girl too. They've just come to steal—"

"I'm not interested in anything you have to say," Talitha said. "Go on, and don't come back until you've a mind to apologize."

More footsteps. Then Harlan burst through the front door. He paused on the porch, his fists clenched, before bounding down the steps. Kit peeked through the vines and watched him thunder across the clearing.

Talitha stepped to the door, her mouth pressed into a tight line as she watched Harlan disappear into the woods. Then she turned, noticed Kit, and managed a smile. "Come meet my daddy," she said.

Mr. Crabtree walked with a limp and leaned heavily on a hand-carved cane. "An old mine injury," he said. "Sometimes the mountain bites back." But his eyes sparkled the same way his daughter's did.

Miss Lucy and Roy joined them, and in the commotion of introductions, Kit dared a glance at the wall beside the stove. Harlan had pasted the columns on the wall, just where Talitha had wanted them. But he'd pasted one of the pieces upside down. A torn corner suggested that Talitha had tried to pull the bad piece off, only to find that the paste had hardened.

Why would he be so mean to Talitha? Kit wondered miserably. *And what does he think Miss Lucy and I are stealing?*

The visit with Mr. Crabtree lifted everyone's spirits. "Sure, my daddy made fine baskets," he told Miss Lucy. "He was the third generation at least who tramped about selling baskets." He stretched out his stiff leg with a regretful smile. "He taught me too, but I thought I could take better care of my family by going into the mine."

Talitha fetched some of the baskets her grandfather had made. They ranged from tall clothes hampers to a basket tiny enough to fit into Kit's palm. "What workmanship!" Miss Lucy breathed.

Kit leaned closer, taking notes as Mr. Crabtree told how each basket was used. The baskets were sturdy and practical, without the surprising artistry of Mrs. Skidmore's baskets made from mixed materials. But as Kit studied them closely, she saw even more clearly how much skill had gone into them. Each basket was perfectly balanced, and the subtle patterns made by the ribs and woven oak splits were beautiful.

"This one is so small," Kit said, touching the tiny basket with a gentle finger. "What was it used for?"

Mr. Crabtree smiled mischievously. "See if you can guess," he said, and recited a verse:

Small enough to cradle,
But big enough to hold
Memories aplenty
As we both grow old.

"Oh, Daddy, don't tease," Talitha said. She looked from Kit to Miss Lucy. "He's always making up riddles."

"A riddle?" Kit thought hard, staring from the old man's grin to the basket. "It was a gift for someone special?" she finally guessed.

His grin grew wider. "I gave that to Talitha's mama the day I asked her to marry me."

Miss Lucy laughed. "Very clever!"

"Oh, I can make up a riddle right outten my head," Mr. Crabtree assured them. "All those years I shoveled coal, I needed something to do. So I'd think up riddles and bring 'em home for the kids."

"We used to hang over the garden fence,

waiting for Daddy to come home," Talitha added, and Kit smiled at the image of a row of children watching for their father.

Since Miss Lucy wasn't able to take photographs of the baskets, she carefully measured and sketched each one. While she worked, Mr. Crabtree shared more of his riddles. Kit guessed some of them, but not all. "Don't tell me the answers," she said. "I'll get them yet." She copied several riddles into her notebook so that she could puzzle them through later.

By the end of the afternoon Miss Lucy had documented fourteen baskets, Roy had already made one trip back to the wagon to check on his horse, Kit's hand ached from scribbling, and Mr. Crabtree was still telling stories about the past. "I got more," he said.

"I'm afraid we should be heading on," Miss Lucy said. She looked frustrated. "I so wish I could have brought my camera! Look, Kit, at the way the sun is slanting through the window. Wouldn't that make a fine portrait?"

Kit could see how the light illuminated Mr. Crabtree's seamed face and gnarled hands, leaving the rest of the room's clutter to fade into shadows. "It would be a fine picture," she agreed.

"Perhaps I can borrow a smaller camera and come back sometime," Miss Lucy murmured. "Mr. Crabtree, would that be all right?"

"Well, I'd be purely satisfied with that." Mr. Crabtree's grin made him look like a little boy. "This is the most fun I've had in months."

"*I'll* come back when I've figured out your riddles, and ask for more!" Kit promised as they headed out the front door. Then she stopped and stared. *"Oh!"*

The afternoon sun was about to disappear behind the western ridge, but its last slanting rays hit the dead tree in the corner of the garden. The empty bottles dangling from its branches glowed with a fiery rainbow.

"That's magnificent!" Miss Lucy breathed.

"My daddy spent too much time in dark

coal mines," Talitha said. "Now I do what I can for him. Sometimes of an afternoon, we sit out here. It's peaceable."

Peaceable, Kit thought as she followed Roy and Miss Lucy back through the woods. Now *that* was a word to collect and remember.

When they got back to the plank bridge, Kit offered to take the satchel from Miss Lucy. "You'll have better balance without it," she observed.

Miss Lucy made it across the plank with less hesitation this time. "I'll go next," Kit said. After settling the heavy satchel's strap squarely on her right shoulder, she stepped out onto the plank. Kit walked carefully, feeling ahead with her toes. This time she knew better than to look down at the creek dancing noisily below. *I could be a famous circus artist crossing the high wire!* she thought, laughing as she imagined trading her thin cotton dress for a fancy sequined costume—

Suddenly Kit's right foot slipped from the plank. The satchel strap slid to her elbow, jerking her further off balance. Kit tried desperately to regain her balance, but in an instant she plunged into the icy water.

The cold almost stole her breath, and the fast current gave her one good tumble before she found footing. As Kit staggered in the waist-deep water, some part of her mind shrieked, *The satchel! Grab the satchel!* She caught a blurry glimpse of its leather strap, lunged, and toppled face-first into the water. Her fingers closed around the leather, though, and she pulled the bag tight against her chest. Shivering and coughing, she floundered to the far side of the creek.

"Are you all right?" Roy called. He had scampered across the plank after Kit fell, and now he extended a hand to help pull her onto dry land.

"Yes, but—but our notes!" Kit swiped cold driblets and hot tears from her eyes. "Our notebooks got soaked! Oh Miss Lucy, all your careful drawings!"

Miss Lucy looked stunned, and it took her

a moment to find words. "We might be able to salvage them," she said.

"I'm sorry." Kit shoved a strand of wet hair from her face. "I don't know what happened. One minute I had my balance—and the next minute I was in the water."

"All that matters is that you're not hurt." Miss Lucy put an arm around Kit's shoulders.

"I'm not hurt," Kit assured her, but her head hung low as they scrambled up the slope to the road. *If I hadn't been play-acting about being a tightrope walker,* Kit thought miserably, *I wouldn't have fallen in.*

Then Miss Lucy stopped abruptly, taking in a sharp breath. "What is it?" Kit asked, following Miss Lucy's horrified stare.

The camera that they had left so carefully in the wagon was lying on its side in the weeds. And square in the road, smashed into tiny pieces, were Miss Lucy's precious glass plates.

7

A MYSTERIOUS LIGHT

"How many glass plates got broken?" asked Miss Myrtle as she began ladling up the stew she'd made for supper. Miss Lucy had already explained how their workday had ended.

"Twenty-four." Miss Lucy sighed, rubbing her temples. "Some were blank, but others held the photographs I'd taken of Vesta Skidmore's baskets."

"And the notes we took at the Crabtree place got soaked," Kit added in a small voice.

"But at least that was an accident," Miss Lucy said. "The other..."

The other wasn't an accident, Kit thought. Someone had dumped the camera from its padded crate in the wagon and broken the glass plates.

Aunt Millie wiped a dribble of spilled stew from the table with a rag. "I can't believe anyone around here would do such a thing."

"I think it was Harlan Craig!" Kit burst out. "He left the Crabtree place while we were still there."

"That's quite a charge, Margaret Mildred," Aunt Millie said sternly. "Do you have any evidence that Harlan was responsible?"

Kit drummed her heel against the leg of her chair. "No," she admitted.

"It could have been anyone who happened by," Aunt Millie said. "I think it would be wise to keep your suspicions to yourself."

"Yes, Aunt Millie," Kit said, but she stared at her hands as she said it. *Fine,* she thought. She'd keep her suspicions to herself… but only until she *did* find proof!

For a few minutes they sat silently, picking at their food. Finally Miss Lucy put her spoon down. "Enough moping," she said. "What's done is done, and I'm not giving up. Fortunately, the camera appears to be in working order. My brother was going to send more glass plates anyway. I'll go down to town tomorrow and see if they've arrived." She frowned pensively, swirling the water in her mug. "My biggest concern is time. I have to catch a train four days from now."

"I'll help you do over what got lost," Kit promised earnestly. "That is... if you still want my help." She held her breath.

Miss Lucy's smile made Kit feel better. "Of course I do!" Miss Lucy said.

"I think you need a new plan," Aunt Millie announced. "You're driving here and there looking for baskets, I'm trying to organize a PTA, and everyone is up to their eyebrows in hard times. We're not being efficient."

"Millie, what are you thinking?" demanded Miss Myrtle. "I know that look of yours."

"We should have a party!" Aunt Millie said.

"A *party*?" Kit couldn't believe her ears. Miss Myrtle and Miss Lucy simply stared.

Aunt Millie hooted with laughter. "You all

look like you don't know the meaning of the word!"

"I think I understand," Miss Lucy said slowly. "You're suggesting that we give your neighbors a chance to meet me in a fun way."

"We can hold it in the schoolhouse," Aunt Millie said. "How about Saturday evening? That's day after tomorrow. I'll make the rounds and let people know, and invite them to bring any baskets they might want to show. Once everyone is gathered, I'll have a chance to talk with more parents about holding classes. You can set up your camera at my old cabin—it's next to the school, and still furnished with table and chairs. Most of all, people can sing and dance and visit with friends."

"You can arrange for entertainment on such short notice?" Miss Lucy asked, a thoughtful tone in her voice.

Aunt Millie flapped one hand. "Oh, certainly! That's not a problem."

"Billy Zale plays a mean fiddle," Miss Myrtle declared. "And when the Hutchins sisters play guitar and sing, everyone's toes start tapping."

The last crinkles of worry eased from the corners of Miss Lucy's eyes. "It's a wonderful idea," she said. "Let's do it!"

❧

Before going to bed that evening, Kit and Miss Lucy examined the notebooks that had been dunked in the creek. "Let's put pieces of newspaper between the pages to help blot up the moisture," Kit suggested.

"Good idea," Miss Lucy agreed. Then her forehead wrinkled. "Where is the other red notebook, Kit?"

Kit frowned. "What other red notebook?"

"I packed two notebooks with red bindings this morning," Miss Lucy insisted. "There wasn't one in the storage crate in the wagon, and I see only one here. Perhaps the other one was in the satchel and got washed away when you fell into the creek."

In her mind, Kit replayed those wet, cold

moments when she was tumbling in the creek. "I really think the satchel was closed when I pulled it out of the water," she said finally. "Maybe whoever tossed out the camera and the glass plates threw the notebook into the bushes."

"Perhaps you're right," Miss Lucy said. "Don't fret, Kit. I can buy extra notebooks in town." She yawned. "I'm heading to bed now. I want to get an early start in the morning."

Kit turned in too, and after the day's excitement, she fell asleep quickly. But it was still dark when she woke with a start. She listened for some sound that could have interrupted her sleep, but heard only the insistent tick of Miss Myrtle's kitchen clock. Kit flopped back on her mattress. The storeroom was sticky-hot, though, and instead of going back to sleep she found herself thinking again about the wet notebooks. *I can't replace Miss Lucy's sketches, but I'll bet I can make out the notes if I try*, she thought. If she could, it would help make up for her carelessness on the plank bridge.

A Mysterious Light

Kit got up and tiptoed out of the storeroom. She paused, hearing Miss Myrtle's light snores drifting down from the second story. Surely the other women were asleep too.

Pale shafts of moonlight helped Kit creep across the floor to the kitchen table without stubbing any toes on the furniture. She was reaching for a lamp when she sucked in a sudden breath and stared at the window. Had she just seen a light outside?

Kit scurried to the open window and cautiously peered out. Yes, there it was again— a small light blinking on the hill near Miss Myrtle's old family cabin. A moment later, the light disappeared.

Then a distant howling sound drifted through the darkness. Kit felt every tiny hair on the back of her neck and arms prickle. *It's just someone out hunting with his hound dogs,* she told herself, but she couldn't quite shake the heebie-jeebie feeling that something was not right beyond the sturdy walls of Miss Myrtle's house.

Should she wake Miss Myrtle and Aunt Millie? Kit debated, every muscle tight, but finally decided against it. She might rouse Miss Lucy, too, and if Miss Lucy had too many more worries or problems, she might leave for good. Kit didn't want that to happen, especially not because she herself had gotten spooked over nothing.

She took one last look out the window. The night was dark and quiet. Kit decided that the notebooks would have to wait until morning after all, and hurried back to bed.

After breakfast the next morning, Kit followed Aunt Millie when she took scraps outside to feed the chickens. "Aunt Millie?" Kit said. "Last night I saw a light out the kitchen window."

Aunt Millie tossed the crumbs from the pan in her hand. Half a dozen black-and-white chickens raced across the yard, clucking in excitement. "Well, that's possible," Aunt Millie said. "Someone hunting, perhaps. The men often run their hounds at night."

"I did hear dogs," Kit admitted. "But that sound seemed farther away."

Aunt Millie smiled. "Everything seems different at night, doesn't it? When I was a girl, I once saw a light out my window. Turned out my father was plowing at night because it was cooler." She chuckled. "He'd hung a lantern from the plow handle."

"Nobody was plowing the wooded hillside out the kitchen window!" Kit protested.

"Heavens, no," Aunt Millie agreed. "But everything looks different at night. A lantern, a flashlight, a bit of moonlight...it's hard to say what you might have seen."

Kit was sure that the blinking light had not come from the moon! But as she started to speak, she noticed that Aunt Millie was staring at the chickens with a preoccupied expression.

Why, Aunt Millie looks tired! Kit thought with a tingle of alarm. She'd never, ever seen

Aunt Millie with red-rimmed eyes and drooping shoulders.

"Aunt Millie?" Kit asked anxiously. "Do you feel well?"

Aunt Millie blinked and straightened at once. "Never better!" she declared. "And, Kit, the next time you see something spooky at night, remember what William Shakespeare said: 'There is no darkness but ignorance.'"

"I'll remember," Kit promised, but as she watched Aunt Millie march back to the house, a new and terrible thought struck. Suppose someone had decided to do something to frighten Miss Lucy—and Kit—away? Had Harlan been creeping around Miss Myrtle's house looking for more books to destroy? Was Aunt Millie starting to wonder if Kit's and Miss Lucy's presence might bring more trouble from someone who thought of them as "outsiders"?

Even if that's true, Aunt Millie probably wouldn't tell me, Kit thought miserably. *She wouldn't want to worry me.*

A Mysterious Light

Kit stood still. The chickens scurried about with their cheerful *cluck-cluck-clucking,* and a woodpecker's call rang from the trees. But Kit could not enjoy the new day. Someone was trying to ruin Kit and Aunt Millie's plans for growing the library, and Miss Lucy's folklore project as well. Time and again, the only person with ample opportunity was Harlan Craig—the boy who *should* have been devoting every instant to work that would keep Fern and Johnny out of the orphanage.

I need to catch Harlan in the act, Kit thought, *or somehow find proof that he's behind all the trouble.* She didn't know how she was going to do that, but she knew where to start.

8
HUNTING FOR CLUES

After a breakfast of fried apples and butter-milk biscuits dripping with sorghum molasses, Miss Lucy saddled her horse. "I may stay in town overnight," she said, "but I'll be back for the party tomorrow evening." She gave Kit permission to use her typewriter. The dunked notebooks' pages were still dimpled and damp, and the pencil marks faint, but with a little squinting, Kit was able to type up her notes from their visit with Mrs. Skidmore.

After lunch, Aunt Millie changed into her sturdy traveling clothes. "I'll talk to everyone about the party," she told Kit. "Do you want to come with me?"

Kit shook her head. "Fern invited me to spend the night. Since Miss Lucy's gone to town, this is my best chance."

Aunt Millie gave Kit a searching glance. "Are you sure you'll be comfortable spending the night with the Craigs, feeling the way you do about Harlan?"

Kit tried not to squirm. "Well, you were right, Aunt Millie. I can't prove that Harlan destroyed Miss Lucy's things."

"Very well, then." Aunt Millie nodded. "Be sure to ask Myrtle for a little something to take along for supper, though."

An hour later, as Kit splashed up the shallows of Lonesome Branch, she found her footsteps slowing the closer she got to the Craig homeplace. She was determined to discover what Harlan was up to . . . but she didn't want to hurt Fern or add to the Craigs' burdens! Finally she stopped, feeling the cold water rushing around her ankles as her worry bounced from Aunt Millie to Fern and back again. Proving that Harlan was making trouble would upset Fern, but ignoring the problem might leave Harlan free to cause more trouble for Aunt Millie! Someone Kit cared about was likely to get hurt no matter what she decided.

If I'm going to be a reporter, I can't back away from trying to find the truth about a problem, she finally told herself. Determined, she headed on toward Lonesome Hollow.

When Kit reached the Craigs' clearing, she saw Fern sitting on the front porch with a butter churn between her knees. She used both hands to work the long dasher handle up and down to agitate cream until it separated into butter and buttermilk. Kit walked up the slope to the garden. She was about to give a shout of greeting when she paused. Fern's chair was angled away from the creek, and Kit realized that her friend was singing as she worked. Fern's voice was sweet and sure and clear as spring rain. She raised the dasher rhythmically, tapping one toe to the beat.

Kit held her breath, enchanted, until the song was over. Fern paused, peeking beneath the churn lid to check the cream's progress, then settled back to begin churning again.

"Hello!" Kit called, waving.

Fern looked startled, then waved back. "Oh—Kit! Come on up."

"I couldn't help hearing some of your song," Kit said. "It was *beautiful!*"

Fern ducked her head. "I didn't make it up myself. It's just an old love song."

"Your voice made me feel all shivery inside!" Kit burst out. "You really could sing onstage!"

But Fern shook her head so hard her hair swung back and forth. "I just sing to help the time go by," she said firmly. "It keeps me from feeling too lonely. It's surely good of you to visit."

"Aunt Millie said I could spend the night, too," Kit told her, and was rewarded with a smile.

Harlan was nowhere in sight. Kit tried to forget him that afternoon, but it was hard. When Johnny asked eagerly if she'd brought him a new book, she thought of the ruined donations while explaining sadly that she had not. When Kit helped Fern gather laundry hanging on the line and noticed how stained and thin Johnny's extra shirt was, she thought of the money the family might have if Harlan hadn't quit his job in the coal mine, or if he worked harder at the farm.

Kit grabbed the opportunity she'd been waiting for after she and Fern had folded the dry clothes. "I can put these away for you," Kit offered. She tried to sound offhand, although a twinge of guilt made her cheeks feel warm. "It looks like Auntie is starting supper. Maybe she'd like your help."

Fern shrugged. "Well, all right. Most of these things belong to the boys. They sleep upstairs."

Kit headed up to the loft. She put the laundry basket on one of the two narrow beds and quickly surveyed the single chest of drawers, a mirror hanging on the wall, a washbasin on a small stand nearby. The room was tidy, and now that she was here, Kit grew even more uncomfortable at the thought of snooping for evidence of Harlan's wrongdoing. Really, what did she hope to find? A diary where Harlan detailed all of his actions?

Still...this was probably the only chance she'd get to look around. And if she lingered for more than a moment, Fern would start to wonder about her. Nudging aside her unease, Kit got busy.

First she looked under the neatly made beds. A pair of worn shoes sat under each, and she spied a set of battered toy soldiers under one of the beds, but nothing more. Kit tiptoed next to the chest of drawers. The picture book she'd loaned Johnny sat next to a hairbrush and comb. Holding her breath, Kit eased open the top drawer. The drawer was almost empty, with just a couple of pairs of socks and one shirt, crisply ironed, lining the bottom. A couple of warm sweaters were folded into the middle drawer. The bottom drawer held only a miner's scarred helmet and carbide lamp, and the heavy shirt and trousers Harlan had probably worn when digging coal.

There was nothing to suggest why Harlan was going out at night. With a deep sigh, Kit closed the drawer and headed back downstairs.

Kit was glad Harlan didn't show up for supper. "Just divide that up three ways," she said with a glance at the ham Miss Myrtle had sent along. When Auntie Craig gave her a sharp look, Kit added quickly, "Don't tell Miss Myrtle, but I don't like her smoked ham. It's more salty than I'm used to."

Johnny showed Kit how to crumble her corn bread into a glass of buttermilk. "It's good that way!" Kit told him, and he grinned. But her heart ached as she watched him gobble his ham and lick his fingers. Fern ate her piece in tiny bites, savoring every morsel.

They ate fresh pawpaws for dessert. "It tastes a little like a banana!" Kit exclaimed after sampling the cucumber-sized fruit. "Do you grow them in your garden?"

Johnny snorted with laughter.

"Fern, go on and take Kit out to show her," Auntie suggested. "Johnny and I can wash up."

Outside, the sun was sliding behind the western ridges. Fern and Kit walked a narrow trail up the slope behind the house. Fern stopped by a small tree. "Oh, good, more ripe ones," she said. "See? They grow wild." She carefully reached for a cluster of pawpaws, their pale-green skin hiding the fruit Kit had so enjoyed. Fern tucked them into her basket. "I guess most folks in Cincinnati have never tasted pawpaws."

"Nope," Kit agreed. "But if you shipped them to the city, I bet people would buy them."

Fern shook her head. "Pawpaws go bad real quick. They'd just turn to brown mush." She carefully picked another cluster of pawpaws. "We do sell what things we can. Ginseng fetches the best price, but it's hard to find. Johnny's good at finding chestnuts and hickory nuts before the squirrels steal 'em all."

That doesn't sound like enough, Kit thought. She felt sick inside, picturing the county worker sending Johnny and Fern to an orphanage, and suddenly she couldn't hold her tongue any longer. "Fern, I don't mean to speak out of turn," she said. "But I—I just can't help thinking that if Harlan would quit roaming about, maybe even doing something bad..." Kit faltered, but forced herself to plunge ahead. "Well, maybe things wouldn't be so hard for the rest of you."

Fern turned her head away. Kit slapped at a whining mosquito, wondering if she'd said too much. Finally Fern sighed. "I'm worried about Harlan," she admitted. "But I don't know that he's doing anything wrong."

"Is he still sneaking out at night?" Kit asked in a low voice.

Fern nodded. "I heard him slip out last night, after it was full dark."

Last night—just when I saw a light near Miss Myrtle's place! Kit thought grimly. "Have you ever followed him to see where he's going?"

"No!" Fern looked shocked. "I'm scared of the dark."

"It would be spooky," Kit admitted.

"And I'd never be able to keep up with him," Fern pointed out. "Harlan's spent his whole life climbing around these hills."

But maybe he won't be climbing the hills tonight, Kit thought. *Maybe he'll head to Miss Myrtle's place to cause trouble.* Suddenly another thought made her catch her breath. She'd seen Harlan sneaking around the abandoned mine, too. What would be a better place to hide a moonshine still than an empty coal mine?

To get to either Miss Myrtle's cabin or the old coal mine, Harlan would probably walk down the stream and then take the road. Trying to think, Kit watched the evening's first fireflies blink up from the grass. Finally she said, "If Harlan goes out tonight, I—I think we should follow him."

Fern worried her lower lip between her teeth, looking unhappy. "He said he had a plan to make some money. I shouldn't meddle in his business."

"But with that county man threatening to take you and Johnny away, it *is* your business!" Kit insisted. "And it wouldn't be so scary if we went together. We could take a lamp or a flashlight along."

"We don't have a flashlight," Fern said. "And lamp oil is too costy. We haven't had any for months."

Kit stared down at the house. She couldn't imagine following Harlan by herself. She would be less nervous about the nighttime forests—and Harlan—if Fern was with her. But if Fern was afraid of the dark…

"Oh!" she said suddenly. "That's it!" She gave her friend a determined nod. "Fern, I have a plan."

9
MIDNIGHT IN LONESOME HOLLOW

Harlan returned that evening as Kit was reading *Robinson Crusoe* aloud, squinting in the fading light. "Evenin'," he said to the group, and continued on into the house.

Kit and Fern exchanged a quick glance. "I can't see well enough to read anymore," Kit said.

Auntie put her hands on her knees and pushed to her feet. "Time for bed all around."

The boys climbed the steps to the loft, and Auntie Craig retired to the small bedroom she usually shared with Fern. The girls spread feather mattresses and quilts on the floor in the main sitting room. There was nothing to do but wait.

As the minutes ticked by, Kit's eyes grew sandy with fatigue. She started to wonder if Harlan had settled down to a sound night's sleep. *Maybe he won't risk going out past us,* she thought. But suddenly Fern silently put a hand on Kit's arm. Kit heard the sound of stealthy footsteps on the stairs.

Kit tried to breathe with a deep, natural rhythm. A board creaked as Harlan reached the main room. He paused, then crept out the front door. In the shadows, Kit could just make out Fern as she put a warning finger against her lips. Kit counted to ten silently, giving Harlan a head start. Then they followed him into the night.

Fern scurried to the corner of the house, listened a moment, then nodded. "He's headed up the path by the pawpaw bushes," she whispered.

"Really?" Kit frowned. Not what she had expected! "Well, you know that trail," she whispered back. "Let's go."

"You have the matches?" Fern clutched the

carbide lamp from her father's mining helmet.

"In my pocket," Kit assured her. "But we shouldn't light the lamp unless we really need to. Harlan would see it."

She led the way. The night smelled damp, and the air was cool. Insects in the trees kept up a steady chorus: *katy-did, katy-didn't*. Bullfrogs added their deep voices, calling for their *jug-o-rum*. Lonesome Hollow seemed a totally different place from the pretty cove she knew during daylight hours. In the moonlight even rows of sweet potatoes and pole beans and corn in the back garden cast bizarre shadows.

"This is spooky," Fern whispered.

"'There is no darkness but ignorance,'" Kit whispered back, remembering Aunt Millie's quote. "Let's pretend we're some of Robin Hood's merry men, traveling through Sherwood Forest."

As they began climbing the hill, Kit stopped frequently to look and listen for Harlan somewhere ahead of them. There was no sign of him.

"He's gone," Fern murmured. "I think we should go back."

Kit shook her head. "Let's at least climb to the top of the ridge."

Something rustled in the underbrush as they passed the pawpaw bush. Kit stared into the dark shadows. Thinking of Robin Hood didn't help chase her sudden shivers away. In Sherwood Forest, Robin Hood hadn't faced rattlesnakes or panthers or mountain men working their secret moonshine stills.

Trees thinned as the girls reached the top of the rocky, windswept ridge. The open sky made it easier to see the landscape. Kit eased around a jutting sandstone wall by the trail and stopped in its shadow. A sudden breeze felt cool on her sweaty skin. The climb had left her panting, and she marveled when Fern stepped silently into place beside her.

The ridge rolled to Kit's left and right, disappearing into the darkness. Had Harlan crested the ridge and continued down the far side? Had he turned one way or the other and headed along the high ground? Was he shrouded in the shadow of one of the looming outcroppings nearby, or already miles away?

She glanced at Fern, who shrugged and spread her hands as if to say, *Your guess is as good as mine.* For a moment they stood still, straining to hear any fading footsteps. Wind sighed through the pines. Kit felt as if she and Fern were alone in all of Kentucky.

Finally Fern touched Kit's arm. "I really think we lost him," she whispered.

Kit sighed. "I'm sorry, Fern. This was a bad idea. I was sure that Harlan would head for the road, where it would be easier to follow him."

"Why did you think that?" Fern tucked a loose strand of hair behind her right ear.

"Well…" Kit hesitated. She'd made a mess of things, and was reluctant to admit her suspicions about Harlan.

Suddenly Fern grabbed Kit's arm. A mutter drifted to her ears. A man's voice—no, two men's voices. They seemed to be coming from farther down the ridge—and they were getting closer. Kit suddenly remembered Aunt Millie's warning: *Men hardened by bad times tend to come out when the sun goes down.*

"Hide!" Fern breathed into Kit's ear. Kit was already frantically looking for a safe place. The outcropping angled back into the earth, creating a darkened crevice beneath overhanging rock. Kit dropped to her belly and elbowed sideways into the shallow opening between earth and the sandstone wall above her. Fern scrabbled in beside her.

"What was that?" The man's voice sounded nearer now.

"I heard it too." The second voice was deeper. Neither speaker sounded like Harlan.

Fern pressed harder along Kit's right side, edging them both deeper into the dark crevice. Kit squeezed her eyes shut as the cautious footsteps grew louder.

"Something's not right," the deep-voiced man said in a low tone.

Silence stretched over the ridge. Kit felt

the cold earth through her thin cotton dress. A pebble pressed painfully into her cheek, but when she tried to ease her face away, she felt the pressure of unyielding rock above her head.

"Well, I don't hear nothing now," the second man said finally.

Go, Kit urged them silently. *Just go!*

But instead of the quiet footsteps she was aching to hear, she heard a little *scritch* of sound. A moment later she caught the faint whiff of tobacco. One of them had lit a cigarette. "I put in a bit of broom corn this year," the low-voiced man said, and Kit miserably pictured the two of them resting on a rock just a few feet away. "Might be able to sell it."

For the next few minutes, Kit listened as the two men talked. Deep Voice said he thought they'd get rain soon because he'd seen a cat washing its ears that afternoon. The other man wasn't sure. And all the while Kit grew more aware of the hard ground beneath her, and of the massive rock pressing down above her, and of Fern pressing close and blocking her only escape. Kit felt her breathing become fast and shallow again, as if she'd just run up the hill. She silently clenched her fists, trying to fend off panic.

Just when Kit didn't think she could stay still for another moment, she heard the scrabble of footsteps on rocks. The men had evidently finished their smoke and were ready to move on. *Stay still,* Kit ordered herself. *You can do it. Just another minute or two.*

Finally Fern rolled away. Kit shoved with her toes and grabbed with her hands, pushing and pulling her way free. She rolled onto her back, wanting to laugh with relief when she saw the moon hanging in the sky. Instead she sucked in a few deep gulps of air.

"They headed up the ridge." Fern pointed with her right hand. "I think they're well gone. Are you all right?"

"I think so." Kit sat up, took one last shuddering breath, and squared her shoulders. "I just got a little spooked."

Fern nodded. "Let's light the lamp."

Kit fished the matches from her pocket. "Yes," she said fervently. "Let's. If those men look back, the light will be hidden by the rock wall."

Once the lamp was lit, the round reflector turned the tiny flame into a warm pool of light. Kit and Fern sat huddled over the glow as if it were a campfire providing warmth and comfort.

"Do you know those men?" Kit finally whispered.

"Probably, but I couldn't tell by their voices."

"What do you suppose they're doing out here?"

Fern shrugged. "Who knows?"

Kit leaned back on her hands. The miner's lamp shoved back some of the darkest shadows, and she could see more of the rock outcropping that sheltered them. "What's that?" She pointed to a crack in the rock wall above her head, and scrambled to her feet for a better look. "Point the light this way."

"I don't see anything," Fern said, but she picked up the light anyway.

"There's something in here!" Kit slid one finger into the crack. A stubby pencil fell out as she pulled free a notebook. It had a red binding.

"Oh my gosh!" Kit breathed. Could this be the very notebook that had disappeared from the supplies left in Roy's wagon? She quickly opened the notebook and was astonished to see nothing but the alphabet, printed over and over on the first few pages. The rest were blank.

"Is this Johnny's?" Kit asked.

"Maybe," Fern said. "He'd do anything to please your Aunt Millie, so maybe he comes up here to practice." But she sounded doubtful.

Kit blew out a disgusted breath. This escapade had turned into a total flop! "Well, one thing's for certain," she said. "Harlan is long gone. Let's head back down to—"

Just then an anguished scream split the night.

10
ANSWERS AND MORE QUESTIONS

The quavering, eerie wail shot through Kit like a jolt of lightning. The notebook fell from her hands. Her hair felt like it was standing on end. Her feet took charge and began to run.

"Kit!" Fern called, her voice still low.

Kit aimed for an open expanse of rock. "Come on!"

Footsteps padded behind her. "Kit, wait!" Fern gasped.

Kit didn't notice the person standing in the shadows of a wind-stunted pine until a hand locked on her arm. Another hand clamped tight over her mouth before she could scream.

"You hush up!" a man commanded in a fierce whisper. Kit kicked wildly.

"Kit, *stop!*" Fern had caught up. "It's Harlan!"

Kit's heart was racing so fast that it took her a few moments to hear her friend. Finally she stopped struggling. Harlan eased his grip enough to let her find solid footing on the ground. He kept his hand over her mouth, though.

"What an *idiot!*" he hissed. "You could break a leg running up here! And anyone in three counties could have heard you!"

Fern grabbed one of Kit's hands. "Kit, we're safe. Promise you won't holler?"

Kit nodded, and Harlan released her. Kit put her hands on her knees and bent, gasping for breath. "But that scream—" she began.

"That was nothing but an itty-bitty old screech owl." Harlan managed to make even a whisper sound mocking.

An *owl*? Kit felt her cheeks burn and was glad of the shadows.

"I want to get offen this ridge before Cy and Lester come back," Harlan muttered. He jabbed a finger in Kit's direction. "You follow now, and follow quiet, or I'll carry you."

Kit glared at him, but nodded. Harlan led the way, and Fern brought up the rear.

Harlan moved with silent grace. Somehow he managed to travel over pebbles and fallen sticks and pinecones without a sound, and to head straight to the path that led down the ridge without needing to pause in the shadows.

Kit shivered as they headed back down the trail. Her dress was damp from fear-produced sweat, her heart still beat too fast, and every nerve prickled. What had Harlan been doing on the ridge? Who were Cy and Lester, and why didn't Harlan want to meet them? What were *they* doing traveling the ridge at midnight?

Harlan set a quick pace, and Kit had all she could do to keep up with him. When they emerged into the Craigs' clearing, Kit was grateful to see the black silhouettes of the house and barn loom ahead of her. Harlan paused near the back garden, then turned to face Kit and Fern. "Behind the barn," he growled, pointing. "We got to talk, and I don't want to wake Johnny or Mamaw."

Once they were behind the barn, Kit found that her knees were suddenly very willing to fold, and she sat down on the ground. Fern dropped wordlessly beside her. Harlan paced back and forth, then crouched in front of them. "Now," he said in a low tone. "What in blazes did you two think you were doing?"

Fern and Kit exchanged an uneasy glance.

"Answer me!"

"Following you!" Kit burst out.

Harlan's tone was sharp as glass. "Why?"

"Because your sister was worried about you," Kit said. "And—and because I wanted to see what you were up to!"

"What I'm up to is no business of yours," Harlan snapped. "You're nothing but a nosy little outsider, come here to cause trouble."

"That's not fair," Kit hissed hotly. "I did *not* come here to cause trouble! And neither did Miss Lucy. I just want to help with the traveling library so people like Fern and Johnny can have books to read, and Miss Lucy just wants—"

"Your Miss Lucy just wants to study the

quaint hillbillies." Harlan's tone was bitter. "Neither one of you is any better than the men who come to steal our timber and our coal."

A flush of anger wiped away Kit's chill. "I'm not stealing *anything*!"

"I've seen you!" Harlan crossed his arms over his chest. "Writing down Mamaw's way of putting up beans. Copying something Fern says into that notebook of yours. You're stealing bits and pieces of—of who we are, just so you can go back home to your big-city friends and laugh about the backward mountain folks you met."

"That's not—why, that's..." It took Kit a moment to stop sputtering. "Fern is my *friend*! I would never make fun of her, or anyone else!"

Suddenly Harlan's rage seemed to leak away. He sank onto the grass, and for a long moment he sat with his elbows on his knees and his forehead buried in his hands. Finally he lifted his face. "Maybe you don't even know that you're doing it," he said. "But I've heard you. You think you can make everybody's life better just by passing out books."

Kit opened her mouth, then closed it again. Was that such a bad thing? She knew from her own experience that stories could make hard times a little easier.

Fern put a hand on her brother's arm. "Kit doesn't mean any harm, Harlan." Then she turned to Kit. "And Harlan doesn't either. He's just seen the way of the world. It's not fun when tourists point at us, or when people call us names." Her voice wobbled. "Or when strangers come and threaten to take me and Johnny away from Mamaw, without knowing one pure thing about us."

For a moment no one spoke. Kit heard bull-frogs calling from the creek, and a mouse's tiny rustle in the grass. Had she somehow done something wrong without even realizing it?

"I'm not writing down things because I think they're 'quaint,'" she said finally. "When I record how people preserve food or make something pretty out of next to nothing, I'm doing it because times are hard at my house, too. Just because I live in the city doesn't mean we don't have to pinch pennies."

Fern nodded. Harlan didn't move.

Kit took a deep breath. "And when I write down something somebody says, it's because the people I've met here have beautiful ways of describing things. I'm going to be a newspaper reporter one day. It seems to me that one of the best ways to help outsiders get to know mountain people is to let a reporter like me be your friend. If you send all outsiders away, you're just making things worse."

"I don't think so," Harlan said flatly.

"Oh, hush, Harlan," Fern said. "Don't be so grumpy. Kit hasn't done anything wrong."

"How about dragging you out in the middle of the night?" her brother countered. "You, at least, should have known better than to walk out in the dark!"

"Why?" Kit demanded, eager to turn the conversation around. "Who are Cy and Lester? Are you running a moonshine still with them?"

"Me?" Harlan sounded genuinely surprised. "Where did you get that crazy idea?"

"Well, I did wonder," Fern said defensively. "Since you wouldn't say where you've been sneaking off to at night."

"I promised Mama I'd never." Harlan sounded hurt. "You know that, Fern."

"Then what were Cy and Lester doing?" Kit asked. "Why didn't you want them to know we were up on that ridge?"

Harlan shrugged. "Cy and Lester are decent fellows, both of them. If they've got a moon-shine still tucked down a holler somewheres, it's just because they got hungry children at home and no other way to feed 'em. But you can't fix to ask a man's doings when he's out in the dark of night. Men in that business travel armed, that's all. I didn't want them stumbling onto you two and getting nervy."

"How did you know we were up there?" Kit demanded.

Harlan snorted. "You two couldn't sneak up on a stump! I heard you come out of the house. I watched you come up the trail."

Kit and Fern exchanged a look. They'd

tried so hard to be quiet! "Okay, okay," Kit said. She was tired of being scolded. "Harlan, you haven't told us where you've been going at night."

He crossed his arms. "And I'm not going to, either. Fern, you just have to believe I've got a plan that will make enough money to hold the family together."

"That's not good enough," Kit objected. "Not—not when—"

"Not when *what*?" he demanded.

The words burst out. "Not when somebody came around to Miss Myrtle's place and ruined all the library books I got in the mail!"

"What?" Fern asked.

Kit sighed. "I didn't know how to tell you, since—"

Harlan jumped to his feet and finished the sentence for her. "Since you thought *I* did it. Well, I didn't."

Kit scrambled up so that she could face him. "Well, other than Fern and Johnny and the mailman, you're the only person who knew about those books. And yesterday *somebody* threw Miss Lucy's camera in the weeds and broke her glass plates into pieces." Kit put her hands on her hips. "Right after you left us at the Crabtree place."

"It wasn't me!" Harlan's voice had grown tight as a fiddle string. "Besides, what happens around here is none of your concern."

"It is so, because I care about Fern and Johnny and your mamaw," Kit insisted. "I think you were so angry when you left Talitha Crabtree's place that you saw a good opportunity to make trouble when you got out to the road and spotted our wagon."

"I did *not* dump that woman's things or ruin your books." It sounded as if Harlan was speaking through gritted teeth. "You can't prove I did!"

"No," Kit admitted. "I can't. But I did see you sneaking through the mining camp when Aunt Millie was holding her PTA meeting at the school. I saw you with my own eyes, Harlan. What were you doing there?"

He stared at her, silent. In the moonlight Kit could just make out the angry set of his jaw.

"Harlan?" Fern asked.

He wrenched away from his sister, took a few steps, then stopped. His shoulders sagged. Finally he came back to the girls. "I was there," he admitted. "I needed to talk to Miss Millie."

"What about?" Fern asked. She sounded perplexed.

"And why didn't you just come to the school like everybody else?" Kit demanded. "Why sneak around?"

They glared at each other, and Kit tried to imagine what business Harlan could have had with Aunt Millie. Had he threatened her? Is that why she'd looked more tired than usual? Kit thought back to the expression on Aunt Millie's face . . . and further back to the light blinking by the old cabin.

Then she thought about the newspaper column pasted upside down in Talitha's kitchen, and the notebook left up on the ridge. Kit's anger seeped away. "We found a notebook up

there on the ridge," she said slowly. "Harlan…
did *you* leave it there?"

Harlan's hands clenched into fists, but he
didn't answer.

"Is Aunt Millie teaching you to read?"
Kit asked. "I think maybe you asked her that
afternoon after the rest of us had left the
schoolhouse. And she agreed to meet you in
Miss Myrtle's old cabin at night."

"Maybe I did," Harlan growled. "And
maybe I found that notebook by Roy's wagon.
But after I left Talitha's place, I tracked through
the woods awhile before circling back to the
road, and everything in the wagon was already
dumped by then. I mean to pay for the copy-
book when—when I can." He gave Kit another
scowl. "I left it up on the ridge so I wouldn't
have nosy people peering over my shoulder."

"Oh, Harlan," Fern said. "Why now?"

"Because I heard that the county is going to
hire a few foresters next spring!" Harlan cried.
"The foresters will teach people how to manage their property so that they can sell some

timber every year but never ruin the land."

"That'd be *perfect* for you!" Fern sounded more hopeful than Kit had ever heard her.

"But you got to know how to read and write for a job like that," Harlan told her.

Kit swallowed hard. "Harlan, I'm sorry I—"

But Harlan had heard enough. Before she could finish, he turned and disappeared into the shadows.

For a long moment the girls sat listening to the bullfrogs. Kit's mind was still tumbling.

"I think Harlan told us the truth," Fern said finally. "He can be rough as a corncob, but he's not a liar."

"I believe you," Kit said, feeling lower than low. "I'm sorry, Fern, if I hurt your feelings. And I'll apologize to Harlan, too—if he gives me the chance."

"He will. And I'm not mad."

"Good." Kit blew out a relieved breath. *But if Harlan didn't do those bad things,* she thought, *who did?*

11

A RIDDLE SOLVED

Kit trudged home the next morning, still regretting that she'd embarrassed Harlan by forcing him to admit that he was just learning to read. And she was still worried that his secret plan to make money—whatever it was—might not be enough to save Fern and Johnny from the orphanage.

She found Miss Myrtle on the porch shredding heads of cabbage to make slaw. "Millie left first thing this morning to tell a few more folks about the party," Miss Myrtle said.

Kit spent the rest of the morning at the kitchen table, typing up notes that had been dunked in the creek. Studying Mr. Crabtree's riddles helped get her mind off her troubles. "Listen to this one," Kit said when Miss

Myrtle came inside with her basin of cabbage. Kit recited:

> *The little man leads us on a great big chase,*
> *The coming of the winter makes a great*
>   *big race,*
> *The man in China has a smile on his face,*
> *And the little ones dance in new shoes!*

"Joe Crabtree was always clever with riddles," Miss Myrtle said. "Even when we were kids."

Kit stared at the typed words as something nudged at her memory. Hadn't she heard someone else mention China recently? She concentrated, trying to think . . . then she smacked her hand down on the table.

"I know what this one is about!" she exclaimed. "I saw roots drying on the Craigs' porch the other day. Ginseng, Johnny called it. One root in particular looked like a little man. And Fern said that ginseng is hard to find but that people in China pay a high price for it."

"Oh my, yes," Miss Myrtle said. "'Sang roots are worth a great deal of money, especially if they're old enough to take that human shape."

Kit tapped her pencil, considering. "If someone was digging ginseng roots to earn money, can you think of a reason why they'd want to keep it a secret?"

"Why, sure!" Miss Myrtle looked surprised. "If you find a good 'sang patch, you can't always dig it up right away, you see. A 'sang plant doesn't make seeds until it's several years old, and it takes another three years for the roots to grow big enough to fetch a decent price. Even if a plant is ready to dig, folks often hold off until late fall, to let the root grow as big as possible."

"If someone finds a new 'sang patch at this time of year, it must be hard to decide whether to dig right away," Kit mused. "If you wait, the roots will get bigger. But if you don't dig right away, somebody else could come along and dig 'em up first, right?"

"Exactly." The sharp scent of vinegar sliced

the air as Miss Myrtle began mixing her slaw. "'Sang hunters are fiercely competitive. The best ones know these hills like the back of their own hands. Don't ever make the mistake of asking a 'sang hunter where he digs."

Kit jumped up and surprised Miss Myrtle with a big hug. Surely Harlan's plan for making money this fall involved ginseng! He was probably tracking down every plant he could find, and waiting until the last possible minute to dig them.

"Hello!" someone called from outside.

Miss Myrtle wiped her hands on her apron. "That's Mr. Tibbets." Kit followed Miss Myrtle out to the porch to greet the mailman.

"Fine day, isn't it, Myrtle?" Mr. Tibbets said as he dismounted. Then he lowered his voice. "And Kit, I have another package for you. Is Millie about?"

"No, she's gone." Kit bounded down the steps to accept the parcel. *This* time she wouldn't give anyone a chance to ruin her new library books!

"Come on inside for a minute," Miss Myrtle told the mailman. "I baked up some gingerbread this morning. It's for the party tonight, but I just might be able to slice off a corner without doing any harm." The postman eagerly followed Miss Myrtle inside.

Kit plopped to the porch steps and tore the brown paper away from her package. A magazine called *Farmer's Home Journal* sat on top of the pile, and she grinned. That was perfect for Roy Skidmore! But when she tried to pick it up, the cover came off in her hand. As she looked through the other books and magazines, she found more damage. A big ink blotch stained the cover of *Heidi.* Scribble marks marred a children's book called *Charles and His Puppy Bingo.* When she looked through copies of *Reader's Digest* and *Good Housekeeping,* loose pages fluttered to the ground.

Kit stared at the contents of her parcel, stunned. Then she noticed a folded piece of paper tucked between two of the books. She picked it up slowly and smoothed it open.

A RIDDLE SOLVED

To Miss Margaret Kittredge,

*When our garden club received your
letter requesting donations for a traveling
library, we knew at once that we must help
the unfortunates. Some of these materials
were being discarded by our local library,
and others had made their way to the backs
of our children's closets. I'm sure the poor
mountaineers will be glad to get them,
and I commend you for doing such good
charitable work.*

> *Sincerely,*
> *Mrs. Preston Williamson*

Kit felt a sick twinge in the pit of her stomach. She was so lost in thought that she didn't
hear Aunt Millie riding up the lane on Serena
until the mule brayed. Aunt Millie dismounted
and looped the reins over the porch railing.

"Whatever is the matter?" Aunt Millie
asked. She sat down on the steps beside Kit.

"Look!" Kit said. She showed Aunt Millie
the books. "I sent letters to Cincinnati, asking

people to collect donations for our library. But all I've gotten are books and magazines that are worn out!"

Aunt Millie thumbed through several of the tattered volumes. "Well, a worn-out book is better than no book."

"But listen to this letter!" Kit read the note aloud. "Don't you think it sounds... insulting?"

Aunt Millie fanned herself with her hat. "I think it sounds as if the Garden Club ladies meant well."

Kit felt tears sting her eyes. "Sometimes meaning well isn't good enough," she blurted. "Sometimes you can hurt somebody's feelings without intending to." And then the words came tumbling out, and she told Aunt Millie what had happened the night before. "I think... I think I embarrassed Harlan," Kit confessed. "Now he's angrier at me than ever."

"In these hard times," Aunt Millie said quietly, "sometimes pride is all a body has left."

"I tried to apologize," Kit told her. "I don't know how to make him forgive me."

Aunt Millie stared at the lacy shadows made by the sunshine pouring through the trees. "Give him time, Kit," she said finally. "Give him time."

"He told us about applying for that forestry job in the spring," Kit said. "But that won't help his family right now! It's hard to understand why he left a paying job at that big mine."

Aunt Millie gave Kit a level gaze. "Have you ever been inside a coal mine?"

Something in Aunt Millie's look made Kit's voice come out very small. "No."

"I think you should ask Harlan about working in a mine before you judge his decision to leave," Aunt Millie said.

"Yes, ma'am." Kit knew the advice was good. But Harlan wasn't likely to answer any more questions.

"Harlan has nothing to feel ashamed about," Aunt Millie added. "And he'd make a fine forester. Why, he could *teach* biology! He just needs to catch up on some things. I'll make sure he's straight on that."

Kit felt a little better. Harlan would surely listen to Aunt Millie.

"And Margaret Mildred," Aunt Millie added tartly, "you're not the girl I think you are if you let a few torn pages and ink marks keep you from growing our library."

Kit thought hard, staring at the library donations. Then she squared her shoulders. "You're absolutely right, Aunt Millie," she declared. "I've got an idea for the party tonight."

"Good." Aunt Millie chuckled and rose to her feet.

Kit stayed where she was. The reminder about the party brought back a lingering worry. She *still* didn't know who had dumped Miss Lucy's camera in the road. Whoever had tried to ruin Miss Lucy's equipment might very well make more trouble.

12

RUINED PLANS

"Where is Miss Lucy?" Kit asked, looking impatiently down the empty lane leading to Miss Myrtle's house. "It's time to leave for the party!"

"She must have been delayed in town," Aunt Millie said.

Miss Myrtle joined them in the yard with a cloth-covered basket over her arm. "You two go on, and I'll wait for her. I know you've got things to get set at the schoolhouse. And take this gingerbread with you—"

"Wait!" Kit cried. She dashed down the lane. The creak and rumble she'd heard grew louder, and after a moment, a wagon emerged from the trees.

"Miss Lucy!" Kit cried. "We thought you

might miss the party!"

The driver set the brake, and he and Miss Lucy climbed down to the ground. "Never!" she said. "And I have a surprise!" She grabbed her driver's hand and pulled him forward.

Kit took her first good look at him. *He looks like Miss Lucy!* she thought. He was younger, and his dark hair didn't have Miss Lucy's eye-catching white streak. But he greeted Kit with a warm smile that felt familiar, as if she was seeing an old friend.

Miss Lucy laughed at Kit's expression. "This is my brother, Peter Vanderpool."

"Call me Pete!" he insisted. After giving Kit's hand a firm shake, he greeted Aunt Millie and Miss Myrtle.

"I called Pete as soon as I got to town yesterday," Miss Lucy explained. "He was able to catch a train from Chicago so he could come to the party."

"You came all the way from Chicago to go to our party?" Kit asked.

"Yes," Pete said, "and I have to head back

tomorrow. But my sister has been telling me about the music she's heard while traveling. I work for a radio station, and I think people all over the country would be interested in folk music from the Appalachian mountains."

"I think you're right!" Kit said, remembering how she'd felt listening to Mrs. Skidmore's song and Fern's dulcimer.

"Pete asked me to be on the lookout for talent," Miss Lucy added. "He wants to put together a radio show that would be staged in front of an audience. I didn't think I'd have time to scout for performers on top of getting my own work done, but..." She spread her hands. "The party presented the perfect opportunity."

"How exciting!" Aunt Millie's eyes danced. "Think of it, Kit. Someone we know might end up on the radio!"

"But most of the people I've met here don't own radios," Kit said. "And there's no electricity!"

"Not yet," Aunt Millie said firmly.

Kit liked that attitude. "What are we waiting for?" she asked. "Let's get going!"

"We can take the wagon," Pete offered.

Miss Lucy darted toward the house. "Give me five minutes! I want to get my camera."

While Miss Lucy fetched her equipment, Pete beckoned to Kit. "Want to see what I brought?" he asked, removing the lid from a crate that looked much like the ones his sister used to haul her photographic equipment.

Kit peeked inside and saw a black box, larger than a typewriter, with a rounded top. Extending from the machine was a hose with a bell-shaped horn on the end. "What in tarnation is that?" she asked.

"It's called a Dictaphone," Pete told her. "It's a machine that will let me actually record people when they sing."

"This is going to be the best party ever!" Kit said. But she crossed her fingers behind her back, hoping that whoever had tried to ruin Miss Lucy's project would stay far away from the schoolhouse that evening.

When they arrived at the schoolhouse, Kit helped Aunt Millie arrange the library donations inside before stationing herself behind the refreshment table in the yard. The adults all claimed to be "full from supper," which left plenty of treats for the children. The camera and Dictaphone were locked safely in Aunt Millie's former cabin next door, and Kit let herself relax as she greeted her friends: Fern, Johnny, and Auntie Craig, Mr. Tibbets, the Skidmores, and all the other people she'd met while traveling with Aunt Millie.

Even Talitha Crabtree came, looking pretty as a daffodil. "One of my married sisters is staying with Daddy so that I can enjoy the party," she told Kit, although she didn't look like she was having fun. Kit wondered if she was worried about her father, or about Harlan.

When a good crowd had gathered, Aunt Millie stepped up on a stool and clapped for attention. "Excuse me," she called. "We'll have music and dancing soon. Right now, though, my niece has an announcement."

Kit helped Aunt Millie step down from the stool and then hopped up herself. "We've been able to gather more books and magazines for the traveling library," she called, "but we need the children's help inside."

Looking curious, the children eeled through the crowd to the school door, followed by their parents. Kit and Aunt Millie had spread the damaged books and magazines on a table at the front of the room. Aunt Millie gave instructions, and soon the boys and girls were at their old desks and hard at work. Fern helped Kit repair book bindings with paste. Johnny carefully erased pencil scribbles. Other children cut out pictures from books and magazines that were too damaged to save and began writing their own stories. Kit had donated her extra notebook to the project, and Miss Lucy had donated two more.

"Is it all right if I write a poem?" one girl asked.

Ruined Plans

"I'm going to write about this puppy!" a boy announced, waving a picture of Bingo.

A man scratched his chin. "Why, this is almost as good as having class!" he said. "I can't spare my boys from chores these days. But every once and again, we could meet in the evening like this."

"Look at my Amy there," a woman murmured, "writing a story."

"This was Margaret Mildred's idea," Aunt Millie said. Kit felt a ripple of happiness as the parents smiled at her.

By the time deepening shadows drove the children back outside, someone had hung lanterns on poles around the side yard. Billy Zale tuned his fiddle, and the Hutchins sisters tuned their guitars. The clearing rang with laughter.

Kit paused near the schoolhouse steps, taking it all in. Then Harlan emerged from the shadows of the lane near the school. This was her chance! "Harlan!" she called softly, hurrying to meet him.

"What do you want?" Harlan snapped.

"Just to apologize," Kit said quickly. "I'm sorry I suspected you of hurting my books and the camera equipment, and I'm sorry that I—"

"Do you think that matters?" Harlan demanded. "None of that matters now!"

Kit stepped back from his quivering anger as someone else appeared from the shadows. "Harlan?" Talitha Crabtree said. "I've been watching for you, and—" She stopped. "What's wrong?"

"Everything is wrong!" Harlan cried. He ran a hand through his hair. "I can't come calling anymore, Talitha. Everything I promised— helping out with your dad, and keeping my family together—it's all ruined."

"But what about your ginseng roots?" Kit blurted. When Harlan stared at her, she explained, "I thought maybe you were going to make a lot of money selling 'sang roots."

"I *was*," Harlan said. "But not now. Someone dug out my best patch!"

"Oh, no." Talitha put a hand over her mouth. Kit could tell that she was the one person whom Harlan had trusted with his plan.

"The roots in that patch were likely worth a hundred dollars," Harlan moaned. "I've been keeping an eye on 'em, taking different routes every day in case somebody was watching. Sometimes I went at night, even."

Talitha shook her head. "It could have been anybody. With money so scarce, more folks than ever are going 'sanging."

"Whoever it was dug every last root." Harlan's voice was bleak.

"We'll get by somehow," Talitha said quietly. "We'll manage."

Harlan's hands curled into fists. "They're going to take the kids away from me and Mamaw."

Kit's heart sank into her shoes.

"I should've dug those plants when I first found them," Harlan said bitterly. "Or just stayed on at the mine."

Talitha stamped her foot. "Harlan Craig, don't say that. You'd shrivel up in a place like that." She turned to Kit. "Do you know he had to go into the mine before dawn and didn't get out until after sunset? For days on end, Harlan never saw daylight."

"That sounds horrible," Kit whispered. She remembered the glorious sunset glow of the bottle tree in Talitha's front yard, and tried to imagine living in constant darkness.

"It wasn't the dark that did me in." Harlan sounded very tired. "It was the noise. The tunnels are shored up overhead with timbers, and all day you hear that wood creaking and groaning with the weight of the whole mountain on top."

Kit remembered something else—that short eternity she'd spent lying beneath the overhang of rock when she and Fern hid from the moonshiners, feeling as if she might never again draw a deep breath.

"We'll figure out something, Harlan," Talitha said stoutly. She curled her fingers around Harlan's. Kit caught her eye, nodded once, and slipped away.

Before joining the crowd, though, Kit took a moment to think. She didn't want Fern and Auntie Craig to hear Harlan's bad news here—not when they were having such a rare fun evening! If only . . .

Feeling desperate, Kit turned an idea over and over in her mind. She needed to talk with Fern. Maybe, just maybe, she could convince Fern to sing for Miss Lucy's brother. Fern would never consent to perform onstage for strangers! But if Pete liked her voice, perhaps Fern could make a recording that he could play on the radio. *We've got to record Fern tonight*, Kit thought. *Tonight is our only chance.*

She was wandering at the edge of the crowd when she found Aunt Millie. "Kit, your idea to have the children work with the donated books was a huge success!" Aunt Millie declared.

"I'm glad," Kit said. "Aunt Millie, have you

seen Fern? I'm hoping I can convince her to sing for Pete tonight."

"I haven't seen Fern in the last few minutes. But I've got good news! I think Miss Lucy is going to be pretty busy tonight." Aunt Millie grinned. "I've talked to several people who brought baskets to show her. As soon as I explain what she's trying to do, most folks are eager to share their stories."

"Maybe you should come out 'in the field' with us, then," Kit said. "Other than Mrs. Skidmore and the Crabtrees, no one wanted to talk to us. Mr. Runyan was especially mean!" She shuddered, remembering the old man's angry threats.

"Now, Margaret Mildred," Aunt Millie reproved. "Mr. Runyan has never had any patience with children. But perhaps you don't know that his wife died a few months ago."

"Oh," Kit said quietly. "I'm sorry to hear that."

"He's miserable, and he takes it out on everybody else." Aunt Millie put a forgiving arm around Kit's shoulders. "I should have warned you and Miss Lucy. Anyone could have predicted that Mr. Runyan would give you a cold welcome."

"Millie!" someone called.

Aunt Millie waved. "Have fun tonight," she told Kit before hurrying away.

Kit stood lost in thought. She wished that Roy had told her about Mr. Runyan losing his wife. He must have known...

Kit brought a hand to her mouth as an unwelcome idea squirmed into her mind. Oh. Oh, oh, *oh.*

"Kit!" Johnny appeared beside her and grabbed her hand. "Come dance!"

"In a little while," Kit promised. "Right now I have to find Miss Lucy."

Kit hurried around the yard, scanning the dancers and the talkers and even the huddle of boys playing marbles in the yellow glow of a kerosene lantern. Finally Kit spotted Mrs. Skidmore, Miss Lucy, and Pete in the center of the crowd. The folklorist was clapping her hands and tapping one toe. Pete looked delighted.

Kit elbowed her way through the crowd. "Miss Lucy! Are the camera and Dictaphone still locked in Aunt Millie's old cabin?"

Miss Lucy looked startled. "I just gave Roy the key so that he could run ahead and unpack for us," she said. "Several people want to sing for Pete, and I—"

Kit didn't hear the rest. She had already started to run.

Aunt Millie's old cabin was on the far side of the school. Kit dodged through the crowd and pelted around the corner, leaving the music and laughter behind her. As she bounded onto the porch, she saw that the front door was already ajar.

"Roy?" she called. She plunged into the cabin. "Roy? Are you here?"

She skidded to a halt when she saw the boy standing at the table, staring at the Dictaphone and camera, his hammer clenched in his hand.

13
THE TRUTH IS TOLD

Kit froze. "Roy, don't do anything with that hammer," she said carefully.

He didn't move.

"Please," Kit begged. "Some of the people Pete records tonight might get hired to perform on the radio. They might get paying jobs! And the photographs Miss Lucy takes could help your mother sell more baskets!"

Brisk footsteps clattered across the porch, and then Miss Lucy and Mrs. Skidmore burst into the room. "Good gracious!" Miss Lucy said, her face crinkling in concern. "Is something happening?"

"Roy?" Mrs. Skidmore asked in an iron tone.

The hammer slid from Roy's fingers and

thudded to the floor. His eyes grew glassy with unshed tears.

Miss Lucy looked at Kit, clearly bewildered. "Do you know what's upsetting Roy? I couldn't imagine why you raced off like that!"

Kit glanced from Roy to the waiting women. She *thought* she knew—but she'd drawn unfair conclusions about Harlan, and about old Mr. Runyan too. She didn't want to make the same mistake now.

Roy gave his eyes a fierce swipe and stuffed his hands into his pockets. "You can tell them," he muttered. "You guessed, didn't you? You know it was me."

"What is this about?" Mrs. Skidmore demanded.

"We had a little trouble a couple of days ago," Kit said. "Someone dumped Miss Lucy's equipment into the road while we were at the Crabtree place." Kit took a deep breath. "Roy went back to the wagon once during the afternoon to check on the horse. He had the perfect opportunity."

"That's ridiculous!" Miss Lucy said.

Kit looked at Roy, wishing her suggestion were ridiculous. "Before that, you'd taken us to Mr. Runyan's place. Tonight Aunt Millie told me about Mr. Runyan being extra crotchety since losing his wife, and I couldn't imagine why you'd taken us there. Aunt Millie also said that most people were willing to help Miss Lucy, once they understood what the folklore project was about. But when you went knocking on doors by yourself, no one was interested."

Mrs. Skidmore put her hands on her hips. "Roy Skidmore. Is this true?"

Roy shrugged, shifting his gaze to the floor, so Kit went on. "Then I thought back to some other things. You wouldn't help Miss Lucy load the wagon when we started that morning, but you offered to help carry the camera over that skinny plank bridge." Suddenly a new thought struck Kit. "And you were behind me on that plank when I fell in! Did you make it wobble?"

"I'm sorry," Roy mumbled. "But I knew the water wasn't deep enough to drown in. I just wanted those papers and things to get ruined."

"But *why*?" Miss Lucy sank into a chair. The change in her expression—from her earlier joy to this look of hurt confusion—twisted Kit's heart.

"Because of my daddy!" Roy burst out.

The sounds of a lively dance tune drifted faintly from the party. The anger in Mrs. Skidmore's face slowly drained away, leaving behind a deep sadness. "I think I can explain," she said with a sigh. "You may have heard that my husband Clete died of illness. But there's more to the story."

She paused. Kit braced herself, already knowing that the story would be sad.

"When Clete lost his mining job, he was frantic," Roy's mother said. "We came back here, and he worked the farm, but it wasn't enough. Then one day we heard that a government aid worker was going to be down in town, hiring men for one of their public projects. Building roads, I think it was. Well, Clete got up long before dawn. I had his best clothes all washed and ironed. When he headed down the mountain, he stepped lively. I saw hope in him that morning."

"What happened?" Kit whispered.

"The aid worker looked Clete up and down and said he didn't look needy enough for the job." Mrs. Skidmore's voice was flat as a slab of sandstone, and just as cold. "When Clete dragged himself back up the mountain, he looked more exhausted than he did after a long day shoveling coal. The next morning he got up and put on his oldest, most ragged work clothes. He rubbed dirt into his hands. He didn't comb his hair. He went back down the mountain and told that aid worker that he hadn't eaten in two days. Clete got hired on without another word."

"Oh," Miss Lucy said. "I see."

"Aid workers have done a lot of good in this county," Mrs. Skidmore said. "But people shouldn't have to beg and lie to get the jobs they need to feed their children. I watched Clete's pride break. The heart just went out of him. When he got sick soon after, I think he just gave up."

"They shamed my daddy," Roy said fiercely.

"Yes they did," Mrs. Skidmore snapped. "But you've shamed me, Roy. There are ways to stand up for what's right, and this isn't one of 'em. What were you about to do with that hammer?"

"I was gonna smash those machines," Roy admitted miserably. "But when I got here... I just couldn't." He hitched one shoulder up and down, staring at the floor.

"He had time to destroy the camera and Dictaphone before we got here, but he didn't," Kit said quickly. "I think he's already having a change of heart."

"Well, that's a start," Mrs. Skidmore said. "But now, Roy, you are going to start thinking about what you can do to make things right by Miss Lucy for the trouble you've already caused."

"I'm sure we can reach an understanding," Miss Lucy said softly. "Now that Roy and I are getting to know each other."

Kit slipped from the cabin with a heavy heart, leaving the others to work things out. *I'm sure that aid worker meant well,* she thought. He'd probably just been trying to make sure that the jobs went to those who needed them most. But helping people wasn't always as easy as it first seemed.

She paused. She still wanted to try to help Fern, but was she doing a good thing? Or was she meddling in matters she didn't really understand?

My idea just might work, she thought stoutly. *It's worth a chance.* With that, she marched back to the party to find Fern.

❧

Half an hour later, Fern stared at the Dictaphone and shook her head. "I don't think I can." She and Kit were in the schoolteacher's cabin with Pete, Miss Lucy, and Auntie Craig.

"You don't have to sing if you don't want to," Miss Lucy said gently. "It's all right."

"She does have the prettiest voice you ever heard," Auntie Craig assured Pete. "Just like an angel come down to earth."

Fern hunched her shoulders. "I'm sorry. It's all too—too strange. I'm used to singing when I drive the cow home and such."

Kit tried to hide her growing sense of urgency. There had to be a way to put Fern at ease! Kit looked desperately around the cabin. Suddenly she jumped to her feet, darted to the corner, and snatched up the short homemade broom Aunt Millie kept there so she could keep things tidy.

"Try sitting in this chair," Kit said, guiding Fern to a seat beside the Dictaphone. "Close your eyes. Now, take this." She pressed the broom handle into Fern's hands. "Remember the first time I heard you sing? You were churning butter. Well, just pretend you're sitting on your own front porch, holding the churn dasher."

That made Fern laugh, but she obediently wrapped her hands around the broom handle. Pete began cranking the handle that operated the Dictaphone. With his other hand, he picked up the small horn attached to the machine by a hose and positioned it in front of Fern. After a moment, Fern began to sing.

When she finished, she opened her eyes and ducked her head, her cheeks stained red with embarrassment. "Well, that's it," she murmured.

Kit held her breath. Pete nodded with a very satisfied expression in his eyes. Miss Lucy steepled her fingers in front of her mouth as she stared at Fern. "My," she said finally. "My, oh, my."

14
NEW STORIES

Ten days later, as Kit stood on Miss Myrtle's porch watching a drizzling rain drip from the roof and tossing crumbs to the chickens, she was astonished to hear a familiar "Hello!" from the trees. Miss Lucy rode up the lane, her horse's hooves *splot-splotting* through the mud.

"Miss Lucy!" Kit exclaimed. "Once you moved on, we didn't expect to see you again!"

Miss Lucy swung down from her horse and joined Kit. Her trousers were soaked and her boots splattered with muck. "I have to leave again tomorrow," she said, "but I had unfinished business here." She scrabbled in her saddlebag, then handed Kit a book. "Can you get this to Roy?"

"*Kentucky Agriculture,*" Kit read. "He'll like this."

"He worked so hard those last couple of days I was here, and he was so apologetic..." Miss Lucy spread her hands. "I wanted him to know there are no hard feelings."

"I'm leaving tomorrow too," Kit told her. "But I'm sure Aunt Millie will give this to Roy."

Miss Lucy nodded. "I brought this for Miss Myrtle." She carefully extracted the photograph Miss Myrtle had asked her to make. It showed Miss Myrtle standing in the yard, her mother's egg basket over her arm. She was looking away from the camera lens, and Kit thought the photograph somehow captured Miss Myrtle's dignity. "It's beautiful," she said.

"*And* I have something for Fern. Pete asked me to deliver it in person. Can you take me to see her?"

Kit took one look at Miss Lucy's joyful smile and whooped. "You bet! And your timing is perfect. Aunt Millie and I were planning to visit the Craigs today anyway."

When the three of them arrived at the Craig homeplace, they found Talitha Crabtree there too, sitting by Harlan. "I heard you were leaving," she told Kit. "I wanted to say good-bye."

They all settled on the sagging porch. "My brother Pete wasn't able to get away from Chicago again," Miss Lucy said. "But he's played the cylinders he made at the party to his boss at the radio station. Fern, they want you to make a record."

Fern's eyes went very wide. "Really?" she whispered.

"Oh, boy!" Johnny shouted.

Miss Lucy pulled an envelope from a pocket inside her coat. "Here's a letter explaining the terms, and some advance money." She handed the envelope to Auntie Craig.

Auntie Craig slowly ripped the envelope open. Her eyes, already damp with emotion, widened when she looked inside. She pulled out a folded piece of paper, then handed the envelope to Harlan. Harlan fingered the green bills inside quickly, his lips moving as he silently counted the amount. His eyes closed for a moment, and he took a deep breath. Then he looked from his grandmother to Fern. "It's enough," he said quietly.

"Hooray!" Kit cried, and jumped up to give Fern a big hug.

Johnny looked perplexed. "Enough for what?"

"Enough to hold body and soul together," Auntie Craig said. She passed the letter to Fern. "There's a paper to sign here. I'll let you read it yourself, but it sounds fair as fair can be." She nodded proudly at her granddaughter. "I always did say you sing like an angel."

"Oh, Mamaw." Fern's cheeks flushed as red as the last cardinal flowers blooming by the creek. "Miss Lucy, we're surely grateful. I'll try to do you proud."

"I have no doubt of that, child," Miss Lucy said. "No doubt at all."

After Miss Lucy answered a few questions about her brother's offer, Fern and Auntie

Craig signed the contract and gave it back to the folklorist. Harlan took the money inside for safekeeping and returned with Fern's dulcimer. "Here," he said, handing it to his sister. *He looks happy!* Kit thought, realizing that she'd never seen Harlan smile before.

The rain picked up, but no one seemed to mind. The earth smelled fresh, and the *pitter-pitter* of droplets on the roof provided gentle accompaniment to Fern's dulcimer.

Kit sighed with contentment when Fern paused between songs for a drink of water. "Oh, Fern, isn't it exciting? I might hear you on the radio when I'm back in Cincinnati. You're going to be a star!"

"Heavens," Fern said. "I don't want anything like that. I'm just glad if I can help out the family, is all."

"You're doing that," Harlan said quietly. He sat in a chair tipped back against the wall. "That advance money will tide us over to spring. I'm still hoping I'll get that forestry job by then."

"I expect you will," Aunt Millie said briskly. "You're a perfect candidate for that position."

Fern shook her head, looking a little dazed. "Everything happened so fast!" She glanced at Miss Lucy, now deep in a conversation with Talitha. "That Miss Lucy. She is a plain one."

Kit wrinkled her forehead. "Do you think so? I think she's pretty!"

Fern looked startled, but then she laughed. "Me too! I just meant she doesn't put on fancy airs."

"Oh!" Kit joined in the laughter. "*Plain.* I'll have to write that down…" Her voice trailed away as she darted a glance at Harlan.

He sighed and shaved another curl of wood from the stick he was whittling. "Go ahead. Write it down."

"I'm going to write a lot when I get home," Kit said. "I want to write a story about everything that happened here this summer." *And then I'm going to read it to the Garden Club,* she thought. She wanted the people in Cincinnati to know how eager boys like Johnny and Roy were to learn, and how Talitha could make a rainbow out of old bottles. She wanted to write about Mrs. Skidmore, holding her family together with basket weaving and determination. And she wanted to write how Fern could just about make the sparrows go still when she sang.

The first hint of autumn hung in the air, so they ate their supper of turnip greens and fried trout inside. After the meal, Talitha and Kit volunteered to fetch wash water. "Talitha," Kit said, as the older girl lowered the bucket into the well. "How long have you and Harlan…"

"Had an understanding?" Talitha smiled. "For a while now."

Kit grabbed the rope to help raise the heavy, full bucket. "I just wondered, because that day when we were at your house, you two had that fight—"

"Oh, that." Talitha waved the memory away like a fly. "Harlan's so smart, I forget how little schooling he's got. I put him in an embarrassing spot, and he got mad. We both got over it."

"Good." Kit nodded.

"Do you know when I decided to marry that boy?" Talitha asked as they started back to the house. "He took me walking up in the hills behind my own place and showed me things I'd never noticed before. He tracked a bee to a honey tree. He smelled some crushed mint and found the spot where a panther had curled up to rest." Talitha grinned at Kit, the damp air making an escaped tendril of hair curl over her forehead.

"That's pretty neat," Kit agreed.

When the dishes were washed, Aunt Millie looked at Kit. "Well, Margaret Mildred, you have a train to catch tomorrow, and Miss Lucy does too. We should head on home."

"Please, just one more song?" Kit begged. She turned to Fern and whispered, "A long one!"

Without any hesitation, Fern fetched her dulcimer and launched into a ballad about a young Englishwoman who dressed in boy's clothes so that she could fetch her true love home from a battlefield.

"Oh," Kit said happily when the last notes died away. "That one tells such a good story."

"I guess there's more ways to tell a story than just books," Harlan said.

Kit gave him a grin. "Yes, Harlan. You're absolutely right."

After that, there was no more stalling. Fern gave Kit a warm hug. "You come back when you can," she said firmly.

"Yes!" Johnny echoed. "Come on back!"

Kit hugged Talitha and Auntie Craig, then stepped to Harlan and extended her hand. "We got off to a bad start," she said. "But I hope we can say good-bye as friends."

"I suppose." This time Harlan's grudging tone held a hint of amusement. "You don't have enough sense to come in from the rain sometimes. But"—his voice grew serious— "you've been a good friend to my sister, and to my family."

"Next time I visit," Kit said, "I hope you'll tell me some of your stories."

Harlan looked startled. Then he nodded. "Might be I could do that."

Kit and Aunt Millie mounted Serena and headed down Lonesome Branch with Miss Lucy. Kit waved over her shoulder until trees hid the Craigs from view. Her mind was bubbling with stories—those she wanted to write, and those her new friends were sending home with her.

Looking Back

A Peek into the Past

A Kentucky mountain home

Kit didn't have to travel far to visit Aunt Millie—her train trip from Cincinnati took just three or four hours. But that short ride carried Kit to a very different world from the city.

The mountains of eastern Kentucky are part of *Appalachia* (ap-uh-LATCH-uh), a region of steep, densely forested hills, rushing streams, and deep *hollows,* or valleys. Well before the American Revolution, settlers began moving into these mountains, where they carved out small farms among the hills and hollows.

For a long time, building roads through this rugged region was nearly impossible. Local people got around just as Kit and Aunt Millie do in the story—by mule or wagon or on foot. Creek beds often served as paths.

Because travel was so difficult, few outsiders or modern changes came into the mountains for many years. It wasn't until about 1900 that railroads finally began bringing more outsiders to Appalachia—tourists, businessmen from mining and timber companies, missionaries, and educators.

These visitors quickly saw that many Appalachian people still relied on skills and traditions that had been largely replaced by "modern life" in other parts of America. Unfortunately, this led many outsiders to look down on the local people as "backward" or "quaint," just as Fern and Harlan explain to Kit.

TOURS IN THE CUMBERLANDS

This 1930s brochure urged tourists to visit Kentucky.

But other outsiders—like the fictional folklore professor, Lucy Vanderpool, and her brother Pete—recognized the beauty and value of Appalachian traditions.

Many mountain musicians used hand-crafted instruments like this dulcimer.

Two researchers collecting mountain ballads around 1910

During the first half of the 1900s, dozens of researchers like Lucy came to Appalachia to study its music, folktales, and handcrafts, such as basketry, weaving, quilting, and furniture making.

Like Lucy, some researchers were most interested in traditions *A weaver at her loom, and traditional woven fabrics* that had been carried on since the time of the early settlers. (As Mrs. Skidmore mentions, one photographer even asked people to pose in old-fashioned clothing, as if modern life hadn't yet touched the mountains.)

A Kentucky basket maker in 1933

In fact, however, many Appalachian traditions did change over time. Researchers like Pete focused on these newer styles of music and crafts.

The work of people like Lucy and Pete boosted Americans' interest in buying Appalachian crafts and listening to Appalachian music and helped create opportunities for some craftspeople and musicians to earn a living from their art.

This kind of research had many challenges, however. Carting bulky equipment over mountain paths was very difficult. One photographer nearly lost her life

A photographer's car stuck in a mountain streambed in the 1940s

while traveling in the mountains—her driver started across a rickety bridge, then barely managed to back up before it collapsed into the deep canyon below!

Researchers occasionally faced another challenge as well—the wariness that some mountain residents felt toward outsiders.

Photographer Doris Ulmann, who visited Appalachia in Kit's time

That wariness grew out of many difficult experiences. In the early 1900s, coal-mining and timber compa-

A Kentucky mountain scarred by mining

nies bought up huge tracts of land, then turned forests and farms into barren hills. The companies provided many jobs, but the pay was low and the work was hard and dangerous. When the Depression hit, many companies closed mines, leaving communities like Mountain Hollow devastated by the loss of jobs, schools, and stores that the company had supported.

Like Fern and Harlan, many people had also felt the sting of outsiders' prejudices. Even outsiders with good intentions often failed to understand the

After a day's work, this exhausted miner is coated with coal dust.

pride, strength, and ingenuity of the people they meant to help. During the Depression, there were many real-life stories like those of Kit's experience with the Cincinnati garden club's book donations, or the government aid worker who broke Mr. Skidmore's spirit.

Over time, however, more and more Americans came to appreciate the arts and traditions of Appalachia. Thanks in part to the researchers who traveled the mountains writing down songs and recording music on Dictaphones and later on albums and radio shows, Appalachian music—especially bluegrass and country—is now a vibrant part of American life.

Appalachian performers in the 1940s and today

AUTHOR'S NOTE

Special thanks to the Kentucky Historical Society folklorists, archivists, and educators for their generous assistance; to the Appalshop staff for making their library of rich resources available; and to Jamie Young for his insights about historical photography.

ABOUT THE AUTHOR

Kathleen Ernst grew up in Maryland in a house full of books. She wrote her first historical novel when she was fifteen and has been hooked ever since!

Today she and her husband live in Wisconsin. Her American Girl books include *Clues in the Shadows: A Molly Mystery; The Runaway Friend: A Kirsten Mystery; Secrets in the Hills: A Josefina Mystery;* and *Danger at the Zoo: A Kit Mystery.* She also wrote three History Mysteries: *Betrayal at Cross Creek, Whistler in the Dark,* and *Trouble at Fort La Pointe.*

Trouble at Fort La Pointe was an Edgar Allan Poe Award nominee. *Danger at the Zoo, Betrayal at Cross Creek,* and *Whistler in the Dark* were all nominated for the Agatha Award.